NORTHUMBE

FOL
TALES

NORTHUMBERLAND
FOLK TALES

MALCOLM GREEN

ILLUSTRATED BY RACHEL EDWARDS

The
History
Press

To the Green Men – Ronald and Joshua

First published 2014

The History Press
The Mill, Brimscombe Port
Stroud, Gloucestershire, GL5 2QG
www.thehistorypress.co.uk

British Library Cataloguing in Publication Data.
A catalogue record for this book is available from the British Library.

ISBN 978 0 7524 8998 8

Typesetting and origination by The History Press
Printed in Great Britain

CONTENTS

Acknowledgements

I wish to thank all those who have read and commented on the stories: Chris Bostock, Holly Clay, Joshua Green, Ronnie Green, Jane Flood, Georgiana Keable, Pat Renton and Katherine Zeserson; Una for being a good childish listening ear; A Bit Crack Storytellers for providing me with opportunities to tell the tales; Linda France for offering me the use of her house and for providing the author photograph for the cover; Burnlaw for being a sanctuary; Coulsen Teasdale for sharing his own tales; the North Pennines Area of Outstanding Natural Beauty (AONB) for commissioning the creation of two of the original tales; a huge thank you to Rachel Edwards for doing all the wonderful illustrations; most especially I want to thank the wide open spaces of Northumberland for nurturing and inspiring me.

INTRODUCTION

I am a storyteller who has been working in the north east since 1984. Many of the stories in this book are my retellings of oral tales or ballads that I have told to various groups over the years. Most have been shaped by a specific place in Northumberland, giving them their own colour and texture. The final three stories are my own invention but they too are inspired by the land, its folklore and the stories of people I met. Researching these tales has taken me to many hidden corners of the county in all weathers, often at dawn or dusk, and these experiences have also affected their final shape.

The special nature of the Northumberland folk tale is a consequence of its location and its landscape. Northumberland is a borderland with a large coastline facing out to Denmark across the North Sea. It embraces the hills of the Cheviots and the North Pennines and has large stretches of moorland with many river valleys. The coastline is largely made up of dunes, with a wide fertile coastal plain and settlements at the mouths of the rivers. It is the least inhabited county in England, with some of the wildest and most remote places. Its border with Scotland and the construction of Hadrian's Wall mean that it also has many stories associated with early English history.

It is the nature of Northumberland's borderland with Scotland that has shaped many of the stories. These lands have been constantly changing and shifting over hundreds of years. They have seldom been fixed for long, often disputed and fought over. They are the debateable lands, liminal lands, lands on a threshold. These lands are not just a threshold between two countries but between two worlds: this world and the 'otherworld', as our Celtic ancestors called it. The lands in and between the river valleys of the Wansbeck, the Coquet and the Aln and into the rugged uplands of the Simonside Hills and the Cheviots are rich with tales of the fairy folk. These fairy folk are found in the place names such as Dancing Hall, Dancing Green Hill, Dancing Green Knowe, Fairy Spring and Elf Hills. They are found in the border ballads 'Tam Lin' and 'Childe Roland', which entice us into this 'otherworld', the fairy world of our imaginations. These fairy characters are not the pretty winged creatures invented by our Victorian ancestors but feisty beings coming out of the land itself.

In this border region you can hardly walk a few hundred yards without encountering a tangible memory of the ancient past in the numerous Iron Age hill forts, Bronze Age cairns and boulders adorned with Neolithic rock art. If you trace these places on a map, it is possible to see a connection between these ancient sites and the places where the stories of the fairy folk are found. The Simonside Hill, known by one archaeologist as the 'sacred mountain', seems to be a locus for many of these stories, with its own tale of the 'Deurgar'.

Northumberland has its own fairy race known as the 'brown men', who inhabit the moors and fells of these northern borderlands. They are distinct amongst English fairies in that they take on the role of protector spirits of the land and its wildlife as found in the stories of 'The Brown Man of the Moors' and 'The Brown Man and the Cow'.

South of Hadrian's Wall, I found far fewer tales of the fairy folk. One fairy, however, that does exist here is a more playful character, the 'Kow', who is intent on playing mischievous tricks, ensuring that people do not take themselves too seriously.

Many of these stories of the fairy folk may have originated with our Anglo-Saxon ancestors or even earlier, with belief systems that revolved around the spirits of the land, when elves were seen to inhabit rocks, rivers and trees. The coming of Christianity challenged belief in these beings. Close to Brinkburn Priory, in a bend in the River Coquet, on top of an ancient settlement and within sight of

Simonside Hill, there is a 'fairy graveyard'. It is possible that this represents the death in the belief of the fairy folk rather than a place where fairies buried their dead. In his Table Book of 1844 Moses Richardson said that 'the little people vanished as soon as the clergy said their prayers at a spot'. Revd John Horsley said in 1729 'the fairies have worn both out of date and out of credit'.

Nonetheless, the belief in the the fairy folk lived on for a good long time in Northumberland. One old Northumbrian man said to Michael Aislabie Denham, a collector of folklore in the early twentieth century, that where he dwelt, 'there was not a solitary hawthorn tree away out in the green hills, standing amidst a circle of fine-cropped grass, that was not witness to a revel and dance between its encircling branches, in the twilight or pale light of the moon'. Auld Nannie Alnwick, a widow of the ancient race of Alnwick tanners in the early nineteenth century, had faith in the 'good folk' and set aside a 'loake of meal and a pat of butter', receiving double in return. She had often seen fairies enter into Harehope Hill and heard their pipe music die away as the green hill closed over them.

Christianity challenged the belief in the fairy folk but brought its own tales. The seventh century was a time of great religious conversions both amongst the kingly class and the ordinary people. Unlike today, Northumberland was a place of great power and influence, with kings such as Edwin and Oswald, both of whom were *Bretwalda*, having over-lordship of many of the Anglo-Saxon kingdoms of Britain. A symbol of their power can be seen in the mighty Castle of Bamburgh, looking out over the North Sea towards Scandinavia. This is the location of the story of 'The Laidly Worm of Spindlestone Heugh'. The kings struggled with the opposing stories of their ancestors' beliefs and the new Christian religion coming from outside. The Venerable Bede (673–735) chronicled many of these tales, so we have the stories of 'Edwin Flirts with God' and 'Crow is Silenced'.

Along with the kings came the great men of Christianity, and none is of more importance in Northumberland than St Cuthbert, made bishop of Lindisfarne in AD 684. He believed in the old

Celtic form of Christianity with its veneration of animals as seen in the stories of 'Cuthbert and the Otters' and 'Cuthbert and the Birds'. It was he, along with St Aidan, of the early converts who persuaded the pagan Northumbrians to join the Christian church, and there are many stories associated with this.

The stories of Cuthbert are, in fact, as poignant in his death as in his life, as his body was carried by a group of monks around the North of England for many years looking for a suitable resting place, safe from the marauding Vikings. The place they finally rested was Dunholme, which eventually became known as Durham, as told in the story, 'St Cuthbert and the Dun Cow'.

The coming of Christianity and these venerable saints did not create peace in these borderlands, so as well as there being many stories of the 'otherworld' there are numerous tales of disputed territory in our above-ground world too.

There was disputation between Scotland and England, but also between families on either side of the border. This was particularly so for 300 years from the thirteenth to the seventeenth century when the border reivers were active. At this time there was near anarchy in the region with big powerful 'reiving' families constantly attacking one another in raids for livestock and wealth. These families had names such as Armstrong, Dodds, Robson and Charlton, and nobody was safe unless they sought protection from one family or another. As a result of this and other cross- border disputes, Northumberland has over seventy castles, more than any other county in England, and literally hundreds of fortified farmhouses and watchtowers known as bastles and pele towers. I have only included a few of the many stories of the border reivers in this book but one of my 'self-penned' stories 'The Gift of the Stone', comes from those disturbed times, as does 'The Hermit of Warkworth'.

Castles, of course, represent wealth, power and land ownership. People who have much wealth to guard have invariably caused some strife in accruing it and very often do not have a peaceful afterlife. So it is in the castles that we often find the stories of ghosts and unquiet souls. There is a string of them just below Hadrian's Wall that echo this, as in the stories of 'The White Lady of Blenkinsopp',

'The Ghostly Bridal of Featherstonehaugh' and 'The Unfortunate Minstrel of Bellister'.

There are tales also that echo the conflict between this big landowning elite, which still dominate much of Northumberland, and the less privileged who live around them. The northern gypsies whose king, William Faa, had his seat at Kirk Yetholm in the Northern Cheviots were one such group. The story of 'The Faa's Revenge' encapsulates well the animosity that existed between these two groups.

It was not just distinct groups such as the gypsies who came into conflict with this elite set but also the village poor, particularly the defiant women who were often branded as witches. It is difficult to know how to tell stories of 'witches', who are usually portrayed as evil but may just be women holding on to a belief in the 'old ways'. The stories 'The Acklington Hare' and 'The Witch of Seaton Delaval' bring this dilemma to light. 'Meg of Meldon' on the other hand appears to be a woman who holds both sides of the coin: a wealthy woman, owning castles, and also branded a bit of a witch.

In Northumberland dragons are known by the Anglo-Saxon name of 'worm'. The story of 'The Worm of Longwitton' poses a similar dilemma to the telling of the 'witch' stories. What is the worm? Could it be the terrifying face of the Viking invaders, the pagan guardian of the well that a Christian knight needed to destroy or something else entirely?

The final chapter of the book includes three tales that are not strictly folk tales but ones that I created from specific places in Northumberland. 'The Gift of the Stone' and 'The Plover's Egg' were inspired by the past history of the village of Blanchland as echoed in an old abbey and the ruins of a lead mine. Both were originally commissioned by the North Pennines Area of Outstanding Beauty. 'The Poacher' was inspired by talking to a farmer called Coulsen Teasdale from Kellah near Haltwhistle about salmon poaching in the 1940s.

I hope you enjoy reading the tales. I have loved writing them. Please read them or, better still, tell them to others.

Malcolm Green, 2014

1

FAIRYFOLK
OF THE FELLS

THE BROWN MAN OF THE ELSDON MOORS

This story takes place on the moors just above Elsdon. It has always been contested land, close to the border with Scotland and near the site of the Battle of Otterburn. On Gallow Hill, overlooking the village, captured Scottish reivers were hung on the skyline. At Winter's Stob, William Winter, a gypsy convicted of murder, dangled in full sight of those passing by on the road. Much nearer to our own time, there were giant placards across the moors protesting against the invasion of wind farms.

Two lads from Newcastle, wealthy enough to be out and about in their caps and tweeds, came to do a spot of hunting on the moors above Elsdon.

They had had a good day's sport, and with their rifles in their hands and a good bag of game tied around their waists they climbed up to the top of Gallow Hill. There they stopped and spread themselves out in the heather to eat their chunks of bread and cheese in the warm afternoon sun.

The younger of the two lads got up and walked down to the Green Glen below to take a drink. He buried his face in the burn and sucked in the clear, sweet water, silently blessing the quiet of the place as he bent down. He raised his head to go when he saw something moving on the other side of the stream. At first his eyes couldn't quite make out what it was and then he saw it: a strange little man staring straight at him. The fellow was strong, stout and camouflaged against the moor with a brown dress the colour of withered bracken and a great cloud of frizzled red hair. The lad realised that he was looking into the face of none other than the Brown Man of the Moors.

They stared at each other in silence for quite some time, the lad becoming increasingly uneasy as the countenance on the little fellow's face became more and more ferocious. But he could neither move nor turn away.

Then eventually the brown man spoke. 'Who do you think I am?' he said in a glowering kind of way.

'You are the lord of the moors,' replied the young man, in a voice that trembled like the reeds around him.

'And what do you think you are doing trespassing on my land?' The brown man said harshly. 'Slaying my creatures without thought or consideration, when all I eat is nuts and seeds.' He waved his hand towards the sprawling vegetation bearing the fruit of the whortleberries, cloudberries and bilberries.

'I meant no harm,' said the young man, fingering his belt. 'I will bring the game over and I vouch that I will shoot no more in your domain.'

The brown man's countenance softened. He beckoned to the young man. 'Come over here and I will show you something.'

The young man was about to jump over the burn when he heard a shout from the bank above. 'What are you doing down there?'

He glanced up and saw his friend waving at him. He turned back to face the brown man but all he saw was an empty moor, the little fellow was gone. The lad scrambled up the hill and told his companion all that had happened.

'It's just as well you didn't jump,' his friend said. 'The water was the only thing protecting you. He would have torn you apart!'

The two lads gathered their things and headed back to Elsdon, shaking their heads in wonder. As they turned a corner in the

path, a grouse sprung up out of the heather in front of them.
The younger lad raised his gun and took the bird down without
thinking. He immediately felt a sharp pain in his side. They
returned to spend the night at the Bird in Hand Inn. After settling
themselves in their room they went to the bar and told their story
to a group of locals. There followed a heated discussion.

'They say those dwarfs eat men,' said one. But another piped up
and said. 'No, they are just there to make sure folks do right.'

Eventually the two went off to their beds. During the night,
however, the pain in the younger lad's side worsened and they
abandoned the next day's shooting to take the coach back to
Newcastle.

Over the following days and weeks, the pain in the poor lad's
side only got worse, despite seeing several doctors. Within six
months he was dead.

THE BROWN MAN AND THE COWT

This story takes place between Keilder Castle in Northumberland and Hermitage Castle in Scotland. Keilder is a place of extremes. It is home to the biggest plantation wood in Europe; it has the darkest skies in England; and it has a mighty lake covering a drowned village. Hermitage Castle, on the other side of the border, however, is a strange and desolate place.

The Cowt of Keilder was a big man, some called him a giant. There was nothing he liked better than to hunt in the wild places around Keilder Castle, returning home with a boar, a stag or a capercaille. He feared little but he did have a rival: the great Lord Soulis, a master of the black arts, who lived over the border.

One morning the Cowt was bridling his horse, calling his hounds, when his wife came to the great oak doors of the castle with a look of distress upon her face. 'Which way do you take your hunt today?' she said. 'Is it eastwards along the Tyne or do you go north to the borderlands?'

'North!' he shouted. 'They say that the game is sweet over there.'

She wrung her hands, 'My lord,' she cried, 'I fear for your life. Lord Soulis would like nothing better than to spill your blood with that enchanted sword of his.'

But the Cowt just laughed. 'Don't fear my love, my own protection is complete, for my helmet is of sand, formed by mermaid's hands and my plume is of rowan leaves. No man can harm me.'

He shouted to his party and they left the castle, journeying through forest and on to the wide open moors. The hunt was on, and the Cowt blew his hunting horn three times. The first time he blew, a curlew shrieked from up above. The second time, the wind dropped to a deathly stillness whilst the fronds of fern still waved wildly over the hill. The third time, a wee man appeared from the thick tangle of heather; his frizzy hair as red as the moor grass, his tunic the brown of winter bracken and a hedgehog on his arm. The brown man of the moors stared at the Cowt with fearsome eyes.

'What business have you here, breaking the silence of the morning and raising the horn for the stag without permission from me? Trouble will befall you, if you continue on your way.'

The Cowt, however, was imperious in front of his fellow men. He brushed the brown man aside and continued up the fell. They rode to the mighty Keilder stone and for good luck and blessing, they rode around it three times sun-wise. On the third time a familiar voice rumbled beneath the stone where the vervian grew.

'Curses on you who ignores the words of the brown man o' the moors.'

An unseen shiver went down the Cowt's spine but still he took no heed and rode on over the border past the birch and the blueberries and into the bonnie brae of Liddlesdale. Approaching Hermitage Castle, a man ran out. 'Lord Soulis welcomes you and has prepared a feast in the hall.'

'Have a fine grip on your swords,' the Cowt yelled at his men. 'For this might be trick or treachery!'

Lord Soulis was surprisingly jolly for an old foe and shook the hand of the Cowt as he entered, 'Take your seats at the table, eat, drink and be merry, you are my guests today.' Red wine slipped down throats, hunting songs were sung and all was merry until suddenly the tapers went out and the party was plunged into darkness.

'It's a trap, take your weapons and flee!' shouted the Cowt. But not one of his men could raise themselves from their seats. They were held fast by Lord Soulis's magic.

Only the Cowt himself, protected as he was by the rowan leaves, was able to stand. With his powerful arms, he carved a path through the throng of Soulis's men and not one of their weapons could pierce his skin. He threw open the mighty oak doors and dashed out on to the moor, plunging his sword down many a throat as he went. A small party stayed in pursuit, amongst them Lord Soulis. But the giant figure of the Cowt led them a merry chase to Liddleswater, beyond which was his homeland. He turned and yelled, 'Soulis, your dark arts cannot touch me!' It was then that the brown man took his revenge. Lord Soulis heard a voice whisper from the heather and glimpsed the face of the red-haired fairy.

'Force him into the water and he will be yours.'

Soulis shouted to his remaining men.

'Into the water with him!' And with their pikes and spears they thrust him off the bridge and under. The Cowt of Keilder's helmet of mermaid's sand, with its plume of rowan leaves was carried away by the current.

All protection gone, their spears entered his soft flesh and the Cowt drowned.

Oh for the folly of ignoring the words of the brown man of the moor!

Lord Soulis and the Redcap

This is a short story that is really an addendum to the above, introducing a new fairy character.

Lord Soulis returned to Hermitage Castle triumphant but here there is another fairy character that enters this story: the little redcap, who inhabits places of tyranny and cruelty, such as castles, bastles, pele towers. Unsurprisingly there was a redcap that lived in Hermitage. Normally redcaps are malign little creatures, looking like old men with large fiery-red eyes, skinny fingers with talons like eagles, matted hair streaming down their backs and iron boots; they are little creatures who take pleasure in hurling rocks at passing travellers and collecting blood in their red caps. The one at Hermitage was a familiar, in league with Lord Soulis, promising his evil master a charmed life, saying:

> While thou shalt bear a charmed life,
> And hold that life of me,
> Gainst lance and arrow, sword and knife,
> I shall thy warrant be.
> Nor forged steel, nor hempen band
> Shall e'er thy limbs confine;
> Till threefold ropes of twisted sand
> Around thy body twine.

But the fairy could not save his master from a pretty dreadful end. For the local people got so sick of his misdoings and cruelty they complained to Robert the Bruce, King of Scotland, who was tired of his wayward vassal and suggested that he be boiled in a cauldron. Whether he meant it literally or not, we do not know, but the people around him relished the challenge. The redcap tried to intervene to save him by ensuring that the ropes to bind him would not hold.

> Redcap sly unseen was by,
> And the ropes would neither twist nor turn.

But the people went to Michael Scott, the powerful Scottish wizard who had charms that were stronger still. And with this power they managed to bind Lord Soulis in lead and took him to the 'old druid's' circle of Nine Stane Rig. Here they mounted a large bronze cauldron on stones in the circle, filled it with water and lit a fire beneath it. They boiled him alive.

> On a circle of stone they placed the pot,
> On a circle of stones but barely nine,
> They heated it red and fiery hot,
> Till the burnished brass did shimmer and shine.

> They rolled him up in a sheet of lead,
> A sheet of lead for a funeral pall.
> They plunged him in the cauldron red,
> And melted him, lead and bones and all.*

It is said that as Lord Soulis was led away from Hermitage for the last time, he tossed the key of the castle over his left shoulder to the redcap so that he might take charge of his hoard of treasure.

---

* Verses included in this tale are taken from John Leyden's ballad *Lord Soulis*, published in Walter Scott, *Minstrelsy of the Scottish Border*.

The Deurgar of Simonside

This story is from the Simonside Hills, a wild rugged area, rich in archaeology and ancient history, with evidence of Mesolithic, Neolithic, Bronze Age and Iron Age settlements. The place is full of intrigue, including a large stone (known as Thompson's Rock) with a 1.7 metre hole running through it which very nearly lines up with the rising sun at midwinter and the setting sun at midsummer. From the summit you can see the Cheviot Hills to the north-west and the sea to the east, with the town of Rothbury nestled in a bend of the River Coquet below. The name Rothbury comes from the Norse 'Hrotha's town'. 'Deurgar' is the Norse name for a dwarf.

It was midwinter and the man in the red jacket left Great Tosson to walk up Simonside Hill. He had left it a bit late to get up and down before dark, but nonetheless, something drew him. He crossed over the stile and walked past the snow-covered mound of the old Burgh fort, his feet crunching over the dead bracken. It was bitterly cold, the northerly wind straining at the bare branches of the rowan trees. He glanced over his shoulder and noticed the white curves of the hills bright in the low sun. The soft track turned into a gloomy path through trees. The snow here was replaced by a shining river of ice. He tried to increase his speed but twice his feet slipped from under him, sending him ignominiously cracking on to the ground. He felt self conscious despite the lack of human witnesses for he felt the mountain was watching his every step. He wasn't long in the forest before he realised he had missed the path to the summit. He would have to make his way to the wood edge and scramble up to Raven's Cleugh. He knew that there was no path but it was preferable to going back.

The snow was deeper here, and he sweated under his heavy garments as he struggled through the heather and on to the large slabs of weathered sandstone. Two ravens croaked above him. From here he could see the bulge of Simonside. The sun was sinking rapidly; it would be set before he got there. 'Damn', a slight flicker of worry. But he had his torch and he should be able to find his way down. The gusting wind rattled a rusty sheep fence; he pulled himself up and started walking more rapidly. He was sure he was being watched.

Eventually he reached the plateau from where he could just see the flickering lights of Rothbury below. Then a mist blew in, as it so often can on these hills, and the view below him was obscured. The man was not worried about it at first but it swirled in thicker and suddenly he couldn't see a thing. He struggled on up the path in the direction of the summit and almost collided with a large pillar of rock. He felt for his torch in one pocket then the next. But he couldn't find it, he had left it behind! A slight panic rose in him. There were nasty precipices here. He would have to wait. He crouched in the lea of the rock. It could easily snow again. He pulled his jacket tight around him, the hood over his head. He wasn't sure if he could survive a night here. He just stared steadfastly into the mist as the last dregs of sunlight disappeared from the sky. A feeling of dread came over him.

He didn't know how long he had crouched before he noticed the light. At first he thought his eyes were tricking him, but he looked again and it was definitely there. He was sure there were no dwellings here but the light was not moving, so what else could it be? He raised himself and cautiously fumbled his way toward it. His hands were numb. The heather snagged his unfeeling feet. But eventually he reached it: a shelter, a small round hut. An animal skin hung over the doorway, allowing the light to escape from a gap. It didn't look like a shepherd's hut, for the shape was wrong. The man carefully pulled the skin back and looked inside. There was a fire and on either side of it a large rock but nobody there. Perhaps it is the hut of a shepherd, an old shieling? Whoever it was, he was thankful. He sat on one of the rocks and held his hands to the fire; he edged his boots as close as he dared without melting the soles. On one side there was a pile of small branches, on the other two large logs. He put a bundle of sticks on the fire and it flared up.

He heard the sound of steps in the snow outside, the door covering moved and in walked a strange being, a person in all but stature, half the size of a normal human. He had rugged features and a tangle of wild red hair. The man shifted uncomfortably, conscious of his trespass, not knowing how to react or what to say. The dwarf went and sat on the rock facing him. The man looked up and was just about to explain himself, when he noticed the dwarf's strange unspeaking countenance, which was neither hostile nor friendly, just completely 'other'. A deurgar, the man said to himself. He shuddered, his tongue silenced. Even if he could speak, there were no words that would come out that would make any sense at all. They sat facing each other in silence. The fire burned down. The man reached out and fed the remaining small branches to the flames. They would not last long. His strange companion continued staring at him, then lent to the other side of the fire and picked one of the logs. The deurgar raised it up and shattered it on his leg. He fed the splinters into the fire, which danced with a million bright, warm flames, painting pictures in the man's mind.

He had no idea how long they sat there. The fire died down again and when he looked up the little man was staring at the one log remaining on the ground. Was he being challenged? There was no way he could break it on his leg the way the dwarf had. He resisted. Silence hung in the air like a stretched skin. He could bear it no more and twisted his body to reach out for the log when suddenly a cock crowed in the valley below. The first smudge of light appeared over the sea. He looked round and the hut was gone, the fire was gone and the deurgar gone. He found himself sitting on top of a bleak windswept rock leaning out into a void, a huge gaping chasm. Another inch and he would have fallen, his body shattered on the rocks below. He shuddered, and then with stiff arms and legs started to walk down towards Rothbury, his whole world spinning. But this time, as he walked, he noticed every step. His eyes and ears were open. He walked past the solar observatory and over the strange spiralling rock art of Lordenshaws. It was all alive in a way he had never seen it before.

THE HENHOLE

This story takes place in the College Valley in the far north of the Cheviots, sandwiched between the great hills of Hare Law to the east and Great Hethra to the west. It is a remote land full of power, contained in the many Iron Age hill forts and a stone circle lying quietly in the valley bottom. The College Burn carves its long, winding way down the valley from the Cheviot Hill, tumbling down the fearsome ravine of the Henhole and snaking its way through moorland, forest and over waterfalls to eventually join the River Till. The valley hums with life; the moorland birds weaving their ecstatic spring dances on the fells and the returning autumnal fish flinging themselves up the Hethpool waterfall. You may also hear high-pitched notes of a hunting horn calling to a pack of hounds as they spread out over the moors on the scent of a fox. Hunting has been happening here for a long time.

Once there was a white stag that graced the woods and pastures of the College Valley. People mostly saw it as dancing shadows or a flash of sunlight through the trees but occasionally it was seen in its full antlered glory, grazing quietly in a clearing.

Nobody could remember quite when it was first seen but as time went on the roebuck became mythical in its presence. Every man wanted to be the one to catch the beast, to have its trophy head mounted on his wall and tell the story of how outwitted it with wile and courage. But try as they might no one could catch it. The stag became the symbol of what every man most desired and none could have.

It was agreed that there would be a mass hunt: the men would spread out across the valley bottom with their hounds and horses and leave no room for it to escape. On the chosen date, one misty spring morning, they assembled outside the little village of Kirknewton. Amongst the gathering were the peasant farmers with their ponies and the noble lords on their fine mares and stallions; there was even one poor stockman with a lame donkey. But no matter who they were, each harboured a dream of glory and honour.

The mist hung low and it was hard to see as the group advanced, slowly fanning out on either side of the burn, each man alert, his heart thumping in his chest. There was an uncanny silence until a voice shouted to the east, 'I have him', and the riders surged in that direction, but almost immediately, there was another voice far off to the west. It was like a held breath. Then all of a sudden the stag appeared; each and every man saw its silken white body leap over the waterfall at Hethpool. There was a gasp, the horns were blown, the hounds barked and the hunt was on, as riders galloped forwards. Those on the large mounts cleared the burn with one jump, others stumbled and fell whilst many detoured to find a shallow crossing.

There was a great commotion, with shouts, yells and the pounding of hooves as riders scrabbled to take the lead, but the stag had disappeared. He was seen by the old mill but no sooner were his dappled flanks glimpsed than they were swallowed by the trees. Men circled.

Then another shout, the stag's lithe form could just be made out bounding through the distant druid circle and up on the flank of the hill below the old fort at Great Hethra. The hounds bayed as they caught the scent once more. The men pounded forward but the stag was soon lost again.

They caught sight of him as he jumped the river again at Fleehope. They blew their horns and urged on their horses with a flick of the whip. The riders were now strung out, the nobles and gentry far ahead on their pedigree steeds whilst the lame-mounted stockman was way at the back, not to be seen. At Mounthooly, the last of the settlements in the College Valley, the white stag burst out of the woods and into that bowl of land leading up the heights of the Cheviot.

There was no shelter here and no going back, only miles of bog before the steep slopes climbed into the hills. The stag's breathing was heavy, sweat poured down its flanks.

The men surely had it now and the leading nobles knew it. The chase was on, each one scented glory. The hounds were gaining on the tired animal, which moved bright as a huge snowflake across the rushes and sphagnum. In the middle of the bowl, the deer paused for a moment, flicked his ears and smelt the air before turning to the east and running straight towards the steep-sided chasm of the Henhole. One noble was in the lead (some say it was Lord Percy but it may well have been long before his time). He shouted, 'The beast's mine,' as he dug his heels into the flanks of his horse, lowered his head and galloped, holding tightly to his lance.

He was only feet away when he glanced up to see the animal spring into the mouth of the ravine. His horse reared up, nearly throwing him off its back and would go no further. The stag bounded up the waterfalls and through the birch trees but try as he might, the noble's horse would not enter that place.

Soon other men arrived on their horses but none would enter. Then one of the farmers arrived. 'That's the realm of the fairies,' he said, 'you'll not be wanting to enter there!' 'What kind of man are you, afraid of the fairies?' shouted back the frustrated noble. 'You'll have to enter by foot,' the farmer replied. But the noble didn't move.

More riders arrived, holding on to their excited mounts, peering up into the chasm but none daring to enter. The sound of the dogs faded into silence. The men were agitated and uneasy, when suddenly a single note of music pierced the air. It floated out of that dark ravine. The horses became calm, the riders strained their ears. What they heard was a sound of great beauty, like a flute played in the atrium of a church. The music swelled until it filled each one of them with warmth. The chill spring day disappeared and was replaced with light, peace and promise. Each man felt a welling up of love. None spoke but, utterly enchanted, one by one they guided their horses into the terrible blackness of the Henhole, mounting the waterfall, winding through the birches until they were all swallowed up.

When the stockman arrived on his lame donkey, all he could see was the prints on the ground. All he could hear was the sound of the wind in the rushes. He rode home alone, wondering the whereabouts of his companions, who were never seen again.

QUEEN MAB'S HILL

This story is from Fawdon Hill, which, like other fairy hills, is a soft, round hill with a hill fort on the summit. The hill is said to be the royal residence of Mab, queen of the fairies. Here she holds her council and settles important matters of the fairy world. In the winter, the view from the hilltop can be stunning with a sky display changing from shafts of radiant sunlight to a smothering blanket of cloud, illuminating and obscuring the hills of Cheviots, Calally and Simonside. The story is found as a poem in the Metrical Legends of James Service.

One day a farmer was riding round Fawdon Hill when he heard silvery music coming from somewhere inside. He rode cautiously toward the sound, to find a door opening into the hill.

He peered through it to see the most extraordinary of sights. There was a fairy court having a lavish banquet. A table groaned with food and wine whilst Queen Mab sat in all her finery at one end with her counsellors seated around her. Musicians held court with their fiddles and flutes. The farmer was literally spellbound, staring into this otherworld, when one of the fairies walked out of the hill towards him and offered him a drink in a silver goblet. In his enchanted state the farmer took the cup and was about to put it to his lips when alarm bells rang inside his head. 'Drink from a fairy cup and you will never be able to leave their world.'

He threw it to the ground and rode off at great speed. He never did see them again or know what it would be like to enter the fairy world.

2

FAIRYFOLK OF THE LOWLANDS AND HOMELANDS

MY AINSEL

This story happens on the hills above Hartburn village in the valley of the Wansbeck. There is a pile of stones here, where a cottage once stood between an old Roman road called the Devil's Causeway and three springs where a dragon once lived.

In its day, the cottage was a simple affair, a single room with stone walls, a heather thatch and a large range. Outside there was a sty for the pig and a vegetable patch. A widow and her young son lived there, for they were poor and the rent was free.

Nobody else would inhabit the place; even the moss-troopers with their lances gave it a wide birth. At least the woman kept it clean and almost free of the invading moss and lichen.

Her front door looked straight up the hillside and the back looked out into the woods that plunged down towards the Hartburn River. There were no neighbours. The only company was the fairy folk that called to each other from the oak trees of the valley sides and the will-'o-the-'wykes that lit up the moors on misty nights and would come tapping on the cottage windows.

The place was famous for the fairy folk. That's what kept the moss-troopers away. Perhaps it was also what made her ten-year-old son so wilful and stubborn. His eyes flashed as blue and as bright as speedwell as he tramped across the moors fearless, looking for the nests of curlew and viper. On midsummer Sunday he would join the village folk by the holy wells of Longwitton, where he listened greedily to the stories being told and dreamt of being a chivalrous knight who wandered the land in search of adventure.

But midsummer was well past now. The nights had closed in and the wind tugged at the door and rattled the window panes. The widow sat by the fire with her son. She swung back the iron arm that held the pot of broth over the fire and said. 'The fairy folk will be out on a night like this. It's early to bed for you and me; under the blankets will be the only place we'll be safe from their chiding and their chatter.'

The boy looked at her. 'I'll not go to bed,' he said.

She argued with this wilful child of hers every night and the battles were getting worse.

'They'll come,' she said 'and you will regret it'.

'I'd be glad if they came!' said the boy, his intense blue eyes staring across the flickering light of the fire. 'At least I'd have some company.'

The woman took her blanket and crossed the room to her bed where she gently sobbed as the house sighed and creaked around her.

The boy stared resolutely at the flames making patterns that drew him into another world of adventure far from here. All of a sudden he heard a flutter in the chimney and a fall of soot. He started. At first he thought 'jackdaws', but this was December, no birds would be nesting now! He held his breath and then, all of a sudden, dangling above the fire was a pair of feet. They jumped deftly over the log and standing in front of him was a girl; a small one, right enough, but definitely a girl, with hair that shone like starlight and red cheeks. Her green eyes stared right into his. She said nothing. In his panic, he searched for words and then timidly he said. 'What do they call you?'

'My Ainsel,' she replied. 'What do they call you?'

'My Ainsel too,' replied the boy, not wanting to reveal more than he had to.

There was a pause. 'Shall we play a game?' she said.

The boy was relieved and picked up a shiny stone from the hearth. He put it in the palm of one hand and held it behind his back.

'Neivy neivy nick nack, which will ye tak?' he chanted.

'Not that kind of game!' said the girl and she gathered ash from the fire and spat on it to make it damp. She began to mould. She made a little cottage, just like his, an old oak tree that towered above, the pig, the deer in the wood with its slender form, the silver salmon in the river. Then very carefully she made people, their bodies, their eyes, their noses, their little ears and she blew a breath into each one of them. The leaves of the tree rustled, the deer began to twitch its ears and ran off into the woods. The people started to move and the boy could see himself.

'What do you want to happen now?' said the girl.

The fire was dying down and it was getting hard to see, so the boy poked the remains of the log to brighten the hearth. A spark flew up and landed on the girl's bare foot.

'YAOOOOOOOW,' she screamed like a wild banshee. The boy leapt across the room in terror, flying into his bed and under the blanket.

Then he heard a grating voice from up the chimney: 'Who's that and what's all the fuss about?'

'It's My Ainsel, my foot got burned,' said the girl.

The boy peeked between the sheets to see a wrinkled upside-down face peer from down the chimney.

'And who did it to you?' it said.

'My Ainsel too,' she replied.

'Well stop the bleating!' scowled the wrinkled face, which picked up the girl with its long bony fingers and whisked her away.

The boy looked across at the hearth and saw the figures crumbling back to ash. His heart beat wildly. 'Well, what did he want to happen next?' He had no idea. But he had never been so glad to hear the sound of his mother breathing beside him. Perhaps she was right: this was the safest place to be.

The following night when she suggested he went to bed, he said, 'Mum, do you want to play a game?' and started scraping ash from the fire.

QUEEN MAB OF ROTHLEY MILL

This story is from Rothley Mill, a scattering of dwellings on the Hartburn, west of Morpeth. The miller is gone and the mill building, scattered stones. But if you look into the river you can see the smooth hollowed out rocks the fairies used for their 'kirning'.

There was once a mill with a heathery roof that sat on the bank of the Hartburn, its black water wheel turning the cogs and millstones that ground the corn. One evening the miller diverted the water from the mill race so that the wheel was still and the machinery silent. He was about to leave when he heard another sound, a bright tinkling, like bells carried on the wind. He peered through a slit in the stone of the mill wall and there, in the gloaming light, he saw small horses deftly making their way through the patches of light on the forest floor. On their backs, figures dressed in green, with their flaxen hair falling over their shoulders. Amongst them was one who stood out, regal and upright. The miller gasped to himself, 'Queen Mab', or was he imagining it all?

A blackbird sang its last notes and chattered off to its night roost. The miller blinked. It was too dark to see their shapes now but he could hear splashing in the river and the chatter of their light voices. The flash of their pale skin in the pools were like bubbles of foam caught in an eddy. He knew they came here and had even left a pick for them to shape their kirns, the hollowed out rocks in which they bathed. Then he heard the melody of the fairy pipers. They were coming in. He gathered a handful of oats for their pottage and husks for them to make their fire. And left them on the 'ogee', or entrance to the drying kiln, where they gathered and cooked.

The miller went out by the back door and walked up the lane to his cottage in Rothley village. It was the first time he had seen them so clearly even though he had known that they came. He was even a little proud: people said the fairy folk came processing over from the Elf Hills to his mill which was the court of the fairy Queen Mab. It was here she held her council meetings. From then on, he left out a little more grain for them each night. In turn the place was kept spick and span. He felt like they cast a blanket of protection over his mill.

Time went on and the miller became prosperous. His flour was good and he had plenty of custom. He had enough money to pay the tailor to sew new suits. He was away a lot and his boys and other lads spent more time looking after the mill. One day, however, he heard them talking, 'the old man is a fool making us leave all that corn for the fairy folk, who does he think they are? We could buy ourselves new shoes for the amount that he gives to them.'

At first the miller felt like barging in and telling the boys 'exactly who they were' but then he imagined their mocking voices and felt slightly stupid. It was a long time since he had worked in the mill, perhaps they were right; perhaps the fairy folk were taking advantage of him. He was not going to look a fool in front of the young ones. He resolved to teach the fairy folk a lesson.

One night he waited until dark and crept on to the newly thatched mill roof. He could hear the tinkle of the bells, splashing in the river and the enchanted pipe music as they entered the building. He bent lower; he could hear their chattering, a thin wisp of smoke came out of the chimney and with it the smell of their pottage. In his hand he had a large sod of turf. He raised it up and hurled it down the chimney, right into their pottage. For a moment there was silence and then one scream followed by another and another. 'Burnt and scalded, burnt and scalded'. And then another voice rang out, 'It was the miller that done it.' Pandemonium broke out amongst the fairy folk inside.

The miller scrambled off the roof and hurried up the road to his house. It wasn't long before he realised he was being followed. He quickened his step but it was still there. He started to run but had to slow down to cross a stile and in his panic, he slipped. At that moment he felt a blow on his back. He looked around and saw the face of the old queen mother of all the fairies. She spat at him and was gone like the fluttering of leaves blown down the path. When the miller got up, he felt a sharp pain that made him wince. He hobbled into the village, clutching his back. It was a wound that never went away and from that day he walked with a limp. Whenever he went near the mill, he heard that terrible voice. 'Burnt and scalded.'

People say that from that day, despite his wealth, he lost heart. Perhaps that is why today the mill is just a ruckle of stones and the gates say 'private'. They say the fairies left and went to Dancing Hall near the village of Lorbottle in the Vale of Whittingham.

If you sit by the river, you might just hear Queen Mab and her followers planning for their return. The Hartburn knows. It heard the story and carried it down to dance and swirl with all the other stories in the river.

THE HOBTHRUSH OF ELSDON

Arriving in Elsdon, you feel like you have gone back in time. It is an almost perfect medieval village nestled in a bowl of hills, with its church, its castle and large village green. If there was ever a place a hobthrush would live it is here.

In the corner of Elsdon by the Motte and Bailey stands the moat house, where a couple once lived. Age was putting wrinkles on their faces and the daily grind of life was getting a little bit too much for them – particularly now it was April and there was the lambing to be done and spring-cleaning to be seen to. The couple looked at each other and shook their heads: the chores just seemed to mount up. What chance had they to finish them?

One morning the old wife woke up, thinking of the mountain of tasks in front of her, chastised the thrush for singing so merrily outside the window and went down the stairs with a heavy foot. But when she entered the living room she couldn't believe her eyes. The grate was clean, the fire was lit, the shoes were polished, the carpet swept and the glasses washed and gleaming. She couldn't believe her husband had done all this, and of course he hadn't. He had his own jobs to do attending to the ewes with their lambs and fixing the broken trailer. So it must have been the neighbours, but as good as they were, they had their own jobs too. So it wasn't them.

It was a mystery, so she kept her counsel to see what would happen on the following days. And it was the same. Each morning she came down, the house was spotless. She took her husband aside and said, 'It must be the little folk'. Now the same thing had been happening to him. His barn had been swept, tools sharpened and wellingtons washed. 'It can't be,' he said. 'Then tell me who it is?' she replied, but he had no answer.

This did not mean that the man and the woman stopped working. They had always worked hard and they always would. But it did mean that their days were easier and there was a little more time to stop and stare and thank the thrush for his morning song. She left an oatcake and a glass of milk in the kitchen each evening and every morning it was gone. Now she was sure it was one of the fairy folk.

Though they were curious, they were careful not to spy upon their helper for they both knew that the little folk do not like to be seen by humans. One night, however, the woman was late home from a friend's, where they had been up into the night making jam for the village fair. As she entered the house, she noticed a candle light in the living room and very quietly she peeked through a gap in the curtains. There he was, the little hobthrush, working away scrubbing the hearth with a spring in his step and a song on his lips. She watched as long as she dared and her heart went out to him, for though he seemed happy enough with his work, his clothes were old and worn. His little jacket was ragged and his hood faded.

She slipped into bed beside her husband. 'I saw him,' she said, 'the little hobthrush, and I'm going to make him a new set of clothes.'

'I hope he didn't see you,' said her husband. 'No, I'm sure he didn't,' she replied, and they both fell asleep.

She was a good seamstress and had noticed well his size and shape. Over the next few days she found the softest and brightest fabrics and made a whole new suit and hood. Her husband even cobbled together a pair of shoes.

The following night she laid them out on the settee with an oat cake and glass of milk, before going to bed. The old woman was fast asleep when she was suddenly woken by an alarming screech. She ran down the stairs just in time to see her little helper disappearing, yelling:

'New cap, new shirt.
This brownie will clean no more dirt.'

The clothes were gone, but the cleaning was left undone and the food untouched.

A golden rule had been broken and the little fellow never came back.

THE HUMSHAUGH PLOUGHMAN

Humshaugh is a small village in a meander of the River North Tyne. Not far away is the only farming family in England that still chooses to plough with horses. You can watch the farmer turning the plough meticulously at each land's end before starting on another furrow.

A man was out one day ploughing a field near Humshaugh in the Tyne Valley. His boy was up front guiding the two horses and the two oxen, whilst he was at the back, holding the plough steady. They reached the 'land's end' when the ploughman heard a great 'kirnin' coming from under the ground. At first he was perplexed, and then he smiled. This was the place the fairies lived, 'they'll be churning their butter' he thought to himself.

There was a sudden 'snap' and a doleful voice said, 'Alack a day, I've broken my kirn-staff, what shall I do?'

The ploughman spoke into the earth, 'give it to me,' he said and carried on ploughing the furrow.

On his next bout he found the staff lying in his track with a hammer and assortment of nails. He stopped his team and in no time at all he had that churning staff fixed and left it back on the ground.

The next time round, there was bread and butter lying in its place. The farmer shared the feast with his whole team. But one rather petulant ox refused to partake of the fairy food.

They set off again to finish ploughing the field before the day was out but as they reached the next land's end the ox keeled over and died.

THE FAIRIES OF GREAT TOSSON

Great Tosson is a hamlet, high up on the north side of the Simonside Hills. It had a number of water mills in the past, with one recorded as grinding corn as far back as 1290.

The miller, Sproat, and his wife, Tibby of Great Tosson, decided to have some time off from the arduous task of attending the mill. They were going to shut the machinery down for the day and visit some friends.

Or at least that's what they thought was going to happen. They were, however, striding off along the steep road toward Rothbury when they both stopped and listened. Tibby was sure she could hear the churning of the water-wheel and the mill gears turning. Sproat walked back to the brow of the hill to check. He turned around and shouted to his wife, 'Tibby, you're right, hen, either the mill has started itself or someone has got inside.' They both looked back aghast. 'Must be some ne'er-do-well up to tricks,' she said, 'we'd better go and see.' They ran back to investigate, cursing their ill-luck.

They arrived and cautiously opened the heavy doors but by the time they entered inside, all was quiet and calm. The stones had stopped grinding and everything was neat and tidy just as Sproat had left it. There was just one thing that caught the miller's attention, the mortar was full of all different kinds of grain'.

'Bless me,' said Tibby. 'There's only one kind of folk that would have done that and that's the fairy folk!'

Sproat nodded and shook his head at the same time. 'Well whoever it was there's no damage done.'

Now, perhaps Tibby and Sproat ever got to visit their friends, perhaps they did not, but Tibby collected up the grain and took it home where she baked the most delicious cake she had ever made.

That evening they shared her fairy cake with the whole family. The dog, however, turned his nose up at it and refused to eat. The following morning he was found stone cold dead.

DANCING ROUND THE HURL STONE

*The coastal plains between Eglingham and Chillingham Castle are
undulating lands criss-crossed with rivers and with an other-worldly
feeling. There are numerous hints of the existence of the fairy folk in
anecdote and place name. One such is the Hurl stone, an extraordinary
twelve-foot leaning stone protruding out of the ground, where fairies
were said to dance.*

George Tate in the *Border Magazine* of 1863 records a time when
explorers descended into the Cateran Hole, some six miles east of
the Hurl Stone and wriggled their way through rock and water
using only candles as lights. They believed they arrived beneath the
Hurl Stone and recount this:

> While resting, [they] were startled by the sound of wondrous music,
> which seemed to come down through the earth above them; the
> strains were wild but entrancing, now rising and swelling, and then
> dying away like the gushes of harmony issuing from the Aeolian
> harp, as the evening breeze fitfully sweeps through the strings when
> other sounds are mute. Ere long, the pattering of tiny feet was
> heard beating time to the wild music; and soon blending with these
> sounds, a song was chanted by many voices, shrill, though sweet,
> but yet unlike earthly tones; and this was the burden of the song:

Wind about and turn again,
And thrice around the Hurl Stane.

Round about and wind again,
And thrice around the Hurl Stane.

The party were terrified – they knew well the dangers of venturing
into the domain of the fairies – and realised they were now
underneath the Hurl Stone, a favourite place of the fairy folk. They
abandoned the rest of their journey and headed home, never to
venture back into Cateran's Hole again.

Round the corner at Chathill Farm children used to dance around a fairy ring but never more than nine times or they knew they would be trapped by the fairy folk.

Fairy Hill A' Alowe

A woman had a child that was remarkably puny, 'but despite all the meat it got within its ill skin, it never grew any'. She feared it was a changeling. One day a neighbour ran in shouting, 'Come outside and you will see a sight. Yanda the fairy hill a' alowe.'

The child suddenly screamed, 'Waes me! What'll become of my wife and bairns!' It sat upright and shot straight up the chimney and out of the house.

3

FAIRYFOLK AND THE MAGIC OINTMENT

THE ELSDON HOWDIE

The magic ointment is a common story motif throughout Britain but Northumberland boasts three versions of it from different villages. The Elsdon story is particularly rich, perhaps because the village has a large village green that was once an important meeting place for drovers. These were men who moved cattle from the sweet pastures of the Scottish highlands to markets further south. As well as livestock they brought with them songs, stories and snippets of news from faraway places. When standing on the village green it is easy to imagine the banter and 'mighty crack', which must have filled the place on the frequent market days.

Margaret sold herbs and medicines in a market stall and it was there she met and fell in love with a drover. At first he was a chancy lad, always away and never home, but eventually he settled down and they were married. He brought with him stories and sweet songs and she her knowledge of herbs and medicines. They were a fine couple but they were never blessed with children, which had been Margaret's heart's desire. She so dearly longed to hold a newborn in her arms and taste the smell of it that she trained as a 'howdie', a midwife. And perhaps because of her longing she was exceptionally skilled at her craft, bringing many dozens of young ones into the world. Her skills were known for miles around and the knocker on her door was seldom still.

Time went on and eventually her bones began to ache and she settled for a life sitting by the fire. She crocheted blankets for the little ones of the village and socks for the old man, her husband, who sat the other side of the hearth. One night she was just about to go to bed, when there was an urgent banging at the door. Someone was in a hurry. She clicked up the latch and outside stood a man, small in stature with a gleaming black horse. 'I've come to fetch you,' he said. 'The master's wife is about to deliver and he has asked for you to come and help with the birth.'

'I'm too old for this,' Margaret replied. But the man insisted, 'The master only wants you and is prepared to pay well.' He held out a capful of gold coins. 'There's the same again if you stay on for a few days and look after mother and child. But you must agree to go blindfolded.'

Now Margaret was intrigued. She understood well enough that folk did not always want their infidelities broadcast, but to be paid with gold! Well she'd never seen the like before; it'd buy a new soft bed and a lot more besides.

'I'll gather my things', she said suddenly.

Margaret got together her bits and pieces and nodded a few words to her husband. The strange man blindfolded her with a silken scarf and mounted her behind him on the horse. They rode out of Elsdon and she guessed, by the movement of the horse, that they took the track along the ridge of hills toward Otterburn. She knew the place well; she had gathered herbs in nearly every nook and dell. Eventually the horse came to a halt. Her blindfold was removed and she stood in front of a grand house on a hill. She looked around in the darkness; she seemed to know the place … but the dwelling? How was it she had never noticed such a fine house before?

The man took her inside where she was met by an old woman, who led her along a corridor with plush carpets and framed pictures on the wall. They came to the room where the soon-to-be mother lay on a four poster bed. The howdie had to stop herself from gasping at the fine drapes, the satin curtains and the warm fire burning in the corner. She smiled at the young woman lying on the bed, who was already in labour, laid out her bits and pieces and set to work. The birth went without a hitch, and the following morning as she was holding the small child, the old woman came in and thanked her profusely. She then looked Margaret in the face and begged her one more favour.

'Please,' she said, handing over a small wooden box. 'Rub this ointment on the child's eyes, our family has a problem and it needs treating twice a day but the medicine is strong, so whatever you do, don't allow it to touch your own eyes.' She paused a moment and said, 'It will do you no good!'

Margaret nodded, intrigued as to what the ointment was. She sniffed it but the scent was foreign to her nose. She did as she was instructed for the next few days and all was well, until one morning when she was applying the ointment, the baby kicked its little toe into her left eye. Without thinking she rubbed it with her ointment-covered finger. She gasped, she rubbed the eye again. She couldn't believe what she saw. She needed to check so she covered the right eye and looked through the left, then covered the left eye and looked through the right. Through the right eye, her normal eye, she saw a beautiful house with paintings on the wall and soft carpets on the floor but through her left eye, the poked one, she saw a damp cave, with moss on the floor and a patchwork of mould and fungi on the walls. Through her right eye she saw a four-poster with fine linen, through her left, a bed of hay and leaves. Through her right a beautiful young woman lay on the bed, through her left, a translucent being with intense green eyes. Through her right eye she was holding a human baby; through her left she was holding a thing from another world, beautiful yes, but strange and haunting.

'So that's why they didn't want me to rub the ointment!' She thought to herself. 'They're fairy folk and it enables me to see through their enchantment.' She bit her lip to stop herself from screaming. She knew she must go now, but leave calmly, so that they did not guess.

She handed the child to the mother, 'She is fine now, I have been here long enough and must go back to my husband.'

'Thank you and be careful,' said the young mother. The old woman got up from the corner and nodded. 'You are free to go, you have done well.' She said and tipped a capful of shining gold and then another into Margaret's bag. The old woman showed Margaret to the door, which to her right eye was solid wood but to her left a worn-out skin. Outside, with her left eye she glimpsed a circle of stones, 'Fawdon Hill' she muttered to herself. Then the blindfold was tied around her once more and she was ridden home. Her husband had told her the old stories of the fairy folk of Fawdon Hill with a twinkle in his eye. He hadn't believed them.

She told nobody of her experience, she was frightened people would laugh at her. But the gold, what would she do with the gold? It was a while before she had the courage to spend it. She walked to the market in Rothbury where she had a fine day buying all sorts of things she had never dreamed of having before. Then there was a bit of a disturbance in one corner. People started complaining about their goods going missing. She looked over and there was a woman, small in stature reaching up and taking rounds of cheese, cream and pats of butter off the stall holder's tables. Nobody seemed to notice her. Margaret shouted, 'Hey you, thief, I can see you!' The woman turned around and Margaret found herself looking into the face of the old woman from the house on the hill.

'Which eye can you see me with' said the old fairy woman. 'This one,' Margaret said, pointing to her left, without thinking.

'That eye has seen enough,' came the reply and the woman moved right up close to her and thrust her long fingernail into Margaret's left eye. It went blind immediately.

She never saw through it again, though she never forgot the fairy folk and knew that though you may not see them, they are there right under your nose!

The Adopted Child of Netherwitton

Through the tiny settlement of Netherwitton winds the River Font, its banks adorned with wild flowers, giving the impression of an enclosed, secret place, away from the world.

There were a couple of cottagers from Netherwitton who lived in a small stone cottage with a garden full of flowers. They had always worked hard but they had never had any children and that had been a great source of unhappiness for them. The man had always longed for a young companion who would help him work the sheep and share his love for the moors. The woman had simply wanted someone with whom she could share her stories.

One day there was a knock at the door, the woman answered and there stood a fine regal-looking looking couple with a boy. The old cottager was flattered that such people should call on her.

'Come in,' she said, you're welcome whoever you are.' The couple stepped inside. 'Please,' she said, 'join us for some tea.' But the strangers declined saying, 'Our time is short and we have business we need to attend to.' The strange man carried on. 'We have heard,' he said, 'that you are good and generous people but that you have never been blessed with children. We would like to strike a bargain with you.' He paused and his wife carried on. 'We have to travel overseas for some time and need someone to take care of our son. We wondered if you would be so kind as to help us out. We will pay you generously.'

The couple sat, amazed, and they glanced at each other, a smile playing over each of their lips. 'Yes of course,' the words tumbled out, 'and there would be no need to pay us but …' 'He is a good lad,' continued the woman, 'and understands the situation, he will give you no trouble.'

'There is just one other thing,' said the strange man. He has trouble with his eyes and needs this ointment rubbed on to them each morning to keep them well.' He handed over a patterned jar with strange inscriptions on it. 'It is strong stuff and would not be good for you, so make sure you don't allow it to touch your eyes.'

So the deal was struck. The strange couple left and suddenly the cottagers had a son of their own. And it was just as they had been told. The boy settled in easily and soon it was as if he had always been there.

The man took him on to the moors where he taught him the whistles for the sheep dog and where to find the nest of the plover. The woman sat by the fire and shared stories and oft-times the three of them sang the old tunes together until it was time for bed.

And as for the ointment, they took it in turns to apply it each day and the jar never seemed to empty. The truth be told, each one of them had moments when they were tempted to try it on their own eyes but they remembered the words of the stranger and held back.

There was one evening, however, just before the fair at Longhorsley, that the man was sitting by the fire, the woman gone to bed and the child dozing, when he glanced across at the strange jar on the mantelpiece. He said to himself. 'What can be the harm in it?' He cautiously took the jar down and opened the lid. Very gently he applied the tiniest of dabs to his left eye and put it back in its place. He looked around and everything was just had it always had been. There was no stinging, no discomfort, and no magic. He forgot about it.

Not long after that the cottager went to the local market to buy some provisions. He was just about to leave when he saw the back of a tall elegant man stretching out and putting articles from various stalls into his bag. The man made no attempt to pay and carried on taking whatever he wanted, without a word being said. Curious, the cottager followed him, watching him put more and more items in his bulging bag.

Eventually he could contain himself no longer and tapped on the thief's shoulder saying, 'What do you think you are doing?' but no sooner were the words out of his mouth than he realised that standing in front of him was his child's father.

'Nothing that you should be seeing,' the tall man replied. 'Which eye do you see me with?' 'This one,' said the cottager, pointing to his left. 'Then you will not be needing it again,' he said, blowing a hot draft of air into the dark pupil, which clouded over instantly.

The cottager struggled to get home that day and when he did, he found his wife crying. Their adopted son had disappeared.

The Doctor and the Fairy King

There is no precise location for this story but it is not far from the Wansbeck Valley, an area rich with the tales of fairy folk.

Once, a country doctor, who lived near Morpeth, was called on by a stranger to visit a patient in the middle of the night. The doctor was understandably reluctant, but when offered gold he changed

his mind and saddled his horse. They rode out into the night, the doctor following the strange man. The places were familiar to him at first but eventually the clouds covered the moon and he became disoriented. They stopped not by a house but in a wild place in the open countryside. The doctor was perplexed but his guide took out a pot of green ointment and instructed him to rub it in his eyes. The doctor did so and immediately the scene was transformed. He saw a magnificent passageway leading to an entrance into the hill. The stranger guided him along a corridor of beautiful lights until he found himself in an underground palace, where he was welcomed by a handsome man who introduced himself as the king of the fairies. Before the doctor had time to think, he was hurried to the chamber of the fairy king's daughter, who was lying in bed with a fever that would not go away. The doctor examined her and found that she had a pip stuck in her throat and could barely breathe. He was a skilful doctor and removed it in no time.

The king of the fairies rewarded him handsomely and insisted the doctor stay for a celebration. After much feasting, a fairy fiddler appeared and set the hall on fire with his playing. Despite his best intentions, the doctor got carried away with the wild dancing and slept in the fairy place. It was evening of the following day that he was eventually led back to his tethered horse. The messenger asked him now to rub a different ointment on to his eyes. The doctor rubbed his right eye and immediately the magnificent fairy entrance disappeared. Thinking that he might like to return on another day, he only pretended to rub the ointment in the left.

A few days later, he went to Morpeth market. To his surprise, he saw a man stealing butter and nobody taking a blind bit of notice. Being a good citizen, he went up to the man and confronted him. The man turned and the doctor saw that it was none other than the king of the fairies. 'So you can see me,' the fairy king said, 'well you will see me no more,' and he blew in the doctor's face. The doctor went immediately blind and never saw ever again.

4

TRICKSTER FAIRYFOLK

THE HEDLEY KOW AND THE LOVERS

The Hedley Kow is a trickster fairy, frequenting the highways and byways on both sides of the Northumberland–Durham border.

Once there were there were two lads set out to meet their sweethearts in an out-the-way location not far from their village. They got to the trysting place but there was no sign of the lasses. Then one lad nodded to the other and pointed out two young women a little way ahead along the road. The lads started walking towards them, in a relaxed sort of fashion, but after a while were surprised to find that they were getting no closer. So they increased their pace, but still the lasses remained the same distance ahead, showing no interest at all in allowing the two young men to catch them up. In frustration, the lads walked even faster but the lasses walked faster too.

The young men, feeling that they were being made to look foolish, decided to put an end to this malarkey and burst into a run. The girls ran too but this time off the road and across the fields. Soon the lads found themselves up to their knees in a deep bog and their sweethearts no longer anywhere to be seen. Instead there was a mocking laugh from somewhere behind and they looked around to see none other than the braying horse's face of the Hedley Kow. Now it was the kow's turn to start chasing them.

The two lads struggled to get through the mire and once freed started to run wildly home. They missed the bridge and had to wade waist high through the Derwent River, the kow's laugh still ringing in their ears. They were now in such a panic that each lad thought the other to be the beast and they ran screaming down the road to their homes, chasing and fleeing from the other at the same time.

They burst into their respective doors and lay down exhausted and shaking. As dawn slowly swept across the sky, each one of them slowly realised that he had been well and truly duped and dearly hoped that their true lasses had not been watching the goings-on that night.

The Hedley Kow and the Black Pot

Hedley on the Hill is a village in the Tyne valley close to the borders of County Durham that is well known for its Kow.

Once there was an old woman who lived at Hedley on the Hill. She was very poor and made a living running errands for farmers' wives. She would get a cup of tea in one house and a piece of meat in another, whilst all the time having a spring in her step and never complaining, which is why people were pleased to see her.

One day she was walking home when it was not quite dark and she saw a big black pot by the side of the road. She looked at it and was surprised, thinking, 'It'd be a fine pot for boiling potatoes; what's it doing here? Perhaps it has a hole in it?'

She walked around it, 'Well if it has got a hole in it,' she muttered to herself, 'it'd be perfect for growing a rose on my window sill.'

She went towards it and gingerly opened the lid. Now that surprised her! It was full of bright, shining, gold pieces. 'My goodness!' she exclaimed quite astonished by what was before her eyes. 'I'd be rich with that, I'd be able to live in a palace and lord knows what else besides.'

Now, with it getting to be dark, there were few folk around to see her and it was too heavy to carry, so she tied her scarf around the treasure to drag it along the road.

She hadn't got far when she needed a little rest, so she stopped and just to make sure, looked inside the pot. But when she opened the lid, what she saw was not gold but a great big block of silver. 'That's strange,' she thought, 'I could have sworn there were gold coins here before.' She smiled to herself. 'A lump of silver, now that is much better than gold, harder to steal or to get lost; I can put it in the corner of my room and watch it shine like the moon.'

So she continued walking, feeling very happy with her wealth. She turned a corner down the long track that led to her cottage but dragging the pot was getting to be hard work so she thought she had better check once more. She opened the lid but what did she see inside but a lump of iron. She scratched her head. 'Iron, I could have sworn there was a block of silver!' She touched it, it was definitely iron. 'Phew' she said, 'I'm so happy. I'll be able sell it easy and make a few coins here and there, without having to worry about explaining where I got it from. I'm so grateful; I'd never have got a decent night's sleep for worrying about that block of silver.'

She walked on and just before she got to the house the woman turned and checked one more time. There tied up in her dusty shawl was a large rock.

'Well I never,' she exclaimed! 'How did it know? It's just the thing I need for holding open my front door to let in the breeze. It's been ages, I've been looking for a rock like that.' She ran down to the house, clicked back the lock on the gate and excitedly opened the door to check how the rock would look in its place. She stared back and the rock was still laying peacefully on the path and she cautiously walked back to pick it up.

Just as she reached down, the rock started to twist and squirm. Suddenly it leapt up and began laughing, 'ha, ha, ha', kicked its hind legs and ran off, very much in the shape of a horse.

The only thing left on the path was her dirty and torn shawl.

The woman, who by now had ceased to be astonished, went into the house and made herself a cup of tea before going to bed.

She smiled to herself and said, 'How lucky am I to have seen the Hedley Kow!'

THE HAZELRIGG DUNNIE

The Hazelrigg Dunnie is a fairy character that frequents a craggy enchanted land just inland from the coast and Holy Island. Here, St Cuthbert's body was said to have rested for a while in a cave at Cockenheugh Crags. There is also the wind-blown Dancing Green Hill, a name that refers to the fairy folk.

It is said that an old reiver frequented the Bowden Doors, a craggy outcrop not far from the village of Hazelrigg. He stole from local farmers and stashed his ill-gotten gains amongst the rocks. A couple of farmers managed to catch the unfortunate man and put an end to him. Some people say that the dunnie that appeared on the rocks was the spirit of that reiver. He would be seen hanging his legs over a crag in the twilight singing to himself:

> Cockenheugh, there's gear enough
> Collierheugh there's mair
> For I've lost the keys o' the Bowden Doors
> An' I'm ruined for evermair.*

The dunnie was then intent on playing tricks on the locals. His favourite was to become the mount that the servant boy used to collect the midwife to attend to a birth. The horse would take the lad to his destination, where the midwife would climb up behind him. On the way back, not far from the house of the birth, the horse would suddenly upend, screaming, and pitch both servant boy and midwife in a mire or a midden and then run off laughing.

The dunnie would do the same to a farmer who had harnessed what he thought was his reliable horse ready to plough a field. He would get going and suddenly the beast would disappear, leaving the man holding on to empty reigns. It was the dunnie striking again!

---

* James Harvey, 'Legends Respecting Huge Stones' in William Henderson's *Notes on the Folklore of the Northern Counties and the Borders*.

5

WORMS, KNIGHTS AND SLEEPING KINGS

THE WORM OF LONGWITTON

This story takes place by the springs of Longwitton, which sit on the top of a steep-sided valley from which they tumble into the Hartburn. On the map they are marked in ancient script as 'Holy Wells'. The largest of the springs trickles out between the roots of an ash tree before carving its way, snake-like down a wooded slope. The waters are chalybeate, full of iron and renowned for their healing properties; the most easterly of them is called 'the eye well'. They were once a sacred place. People came from miles around to celebrate 'Midsummer Sunday'. They would leap over the springs and divine their futures. They would bathe and drink the water, sing songs, tell stories, play games and eat gingerbread. Today, however, no path goes there and it is a forlorn place, surrounded by a trough full of stagnant water, crumbling buildings and rusty machinery. The view down into the valley and over the surrounding hills is, however, magical, and if you linger at the place you can still feel its potent presence. Worm *is the old English word for a dragon.*

A young ploughboy, returning from the fields after a hot sweaty day, made his way to the wells of Longwitton to drink and bathe in its healing waters before he went home.

As he neared the wood edge he saw a flickering shape in the evening light. It was moving by the well. He rubbed his eyes but it was still there. Through the tangle of trees and low sun he could see a large, unfamiliar shape and what looked like a blood-red eye. He froze, his heart pounding. His instinct was to run but also he wanted to see better for the story he would have to tell. A kite circled overhead watching. The ploughboy got on his hands and knees then crept a little closer. He could make out scales, a long neck and a flickering tongue. A stick cracked under his foot and the beast swung its head around, and the ploughboy found his blue eyes staring deep into the red eyes of a dragon. He felt both amazement and terror. But no sooner did he see it than the creature was gone. There was a thudding on the ground and a breath of hot air but no beast.

The boy fled straight to the inn at Hartburn, where his story tumbled out to the astonished crowd. They were minded to think him mad but the tangle of his hair, the colour of his face and the torrent of words convinced the company that it was worth investigating. Dark was already gathering, so they waited until early morning before they ventured forth with their sticks and cudgels.

The men hid amongst the trees on the way to the wells before they ventured closer. They saw nothing at first and wondered if the boy had been imagining it all. But then the birds stopped singing and the wood went so silent it made them shiver. Each man felt a low thud shake the ground, heard branches snapping from trees and saw hot air scorch the leaves. Fear overtook them and they all turned and ran hollering back to the village. Word spread from Morpeth to Mitford and from Mitford to Netherwitton. There was a fearsome beast at the well.

From that day nobody came to the healing wells and the ploughboy took a detour on his way home from the fields.

One day a knight arrived at Longwitton looking for adventure. He swore that he would kill the dragon to prove his worth for God and country. He sharpened his sword and polished his armour and set out for the springs. When he got there he could see nothing. But as he approached the ground shook, the trees around the springs trembled and he felt a hot blast of air in his face.

The knight had been to foreign parts where he had learned the power of charms. He stopped and spoke the words that must be heard, demanding that the beast reveal itself. Slowly the dragon appeared, bringing to light its rainbow scales, its flickering tongue, its fiery breath and a tail that followed the path of the stream from the spring to the river. It lay there and did not move. After all, it had been there for a very long time. The chivalrous knight leapt forwards. He drew his sword and taunted the beast but still it lay motionless. He swung at it, slicing into the skin above a leg. Dragon's blood dripped on the earth and a low roar came into its throat.

The knight stepped back and the dragon raised itself from the ground. For the rest of the day knight and dragon parried with one another around the spring that tumbled into the burn. The trees shook and the buzzard watched from its perch, but by the day's end whatever wounds the iron of our knight's sword had inflicted on the beast were healed. The dragon curled its body back round the spring. The exhausted knight returned to his lodgings swearing that the following day he would fight harder.

The next day he came full of fury. He shouted at the dragon and threw himself, with all his valour and ferocity, on the beast. All day they tangled, striking blows one against the other. The dragon clawed through his armour and the knight struck again and again. Even then, the *worm* would not be overcome. It seemed that all it wanted to do was curl back around its beloved spring. As the knight finally retreated, he glanced back and realised something. The dragon's tail never left the water. Suddenly he understood: it was the water of the healing spring that pumped through its blood.

The third day the knight came with a different strategy. He would use his brain rather than his brawn. He tied up his horse some distance away and, instead of flinging himself into the attack as he had done on the previous days, goaded the beast away from the spring and towards his horse. He parried and stepped back, chiding the beast with words and retreating, further and further until it was some distance from its spring. He then lunged at its throat with his sword, leapt on his horse and put himself between the dragon and the water. The dragon tried with all its might to return but the knight raised his sword and plunged it into the animal's heart. There was no spring to heal the wounds and the dragon trembled, its mighty body falling to the ground. The knight returned victorious. The Worm of Longwitton defeated … for then at least.

Today, people round about Longwitton know little about the springs or the dragon but the landowner did mention that the adjacent field was called the 'dragon field' and that there was a cave by the river called the 'dragon's den', made by a priest for lady swimmers to change in. So the dragon was gone but not forgotten.

The Laidly Worm of Spindlestone Heugh

Bamburgh and the nearby Spindlestone Heugh are dramatic places along a wild coastline facing out to the North Sea. The story was originally a ballad collected by Revd Robert Lambert in 1778. However, its origins may go back to the sixth century when Spindlestone was a site of pagan worship and maidens thrown into the sea as offerings to the gods. King Ida, the first Anglo-Saxon king of Northumberland, was said to have been enchanted by one such maiden, a Bethoc witch with green eyes and dark hair.

There was once a king of Bamburgh Castle whose wife had died, leaving him with a son, Childe Wynd, and a daughter, Margaret. The two of them played in the sands below the castle with the vast, bleak North Sea as their companion, ever enticing them to dream of distant places.

One day Childe Wynd announced that he was going to explore the land beyond the horizon and see what treasure he might find. He embraced his sister, saying, 'I shall return soon with great gifts for you that will make you the most beautiful woman on earth.'

'Be bold my brother, I am waiting for you,' she replied.

But the truth was that Margaret was already the most beautiful of women, with yellow hair that rippled down her back like autumn corn and eyes that sparkled as blue as summer flax. People were proud to have her as their princess and she, in turn, had time for everyone. It was she who controlled the mighty keys to the castle.

Her father, a king of great power, one day announced that he would be away for some time. Margaret looked into his eyes and understood that soon there would be a new queen. She wished him farewell and assumed charge of the castle. Margaret's stature grew as she walked through the streets of the town, a smile on her lips and her body swaying like the sea itself. She greeted everyone from the peasant farmers to the local chieftains, listening to difficulties and resolving disputes. She was particularly courteous to the native Britons, who mistrusted their Anglo-Saxon rulers.

One day came news came of the king's return. People lined the streets, straining to see the carriage as it mounted the steep path to the castle gates. They clicked their tongues with appreciation when they caught glimpses of the new bride, finely dressed with dark skin, black hair and green eyes. Margaret stood by the castle gates, firm and gracious, with two of her loyal local chieftains standing by her side. They cheered as the carriage approached. Then one of the chiefs looked into the green eyes of the new woman and turned to his companion saying, 'She may be beautiful but I don't care for her as I do our Lady Margaret.'

Amongst the hubbub the new queen read the chief's lips and understood much; she immediately felt her authority was threatened. 'Well, your beautiful Margaret will not last for long,' she muttered to herself.

Margaret curtseyed to the new queen as she alighted from the carriage at the castle doors.

'The castle is yours, mother,' she said sweetly as she handed over the keys.

'Thank you, my dear,' replied the new queen, making Margaret feel slightly nervous with the strained smile on her tight lips.

The king noticed nothing of the exchange. He was too entranced by the beauty of his new wife to have any notion that she was a practitioner of the black arts.

The new queen decided to take matters in hand and ensure her authority that very night. She knew that questions would be asked if she simply poisoned the princess, so she decided to deal with Margaret by other means. No sooner had she been shown her room than she unlaced a worn bull's skin bag and took out various phials from which she prepared a concoction. When she was finished, she poured the potion into a small glass jar, leaned over and muttered the words of a charm. She carefully slipped it into her bodice.

That evening, at their very first dinner together the new queen waited until the company's attention was drawn to a convenient altercation in the corridor and poured the liquid into Margaret's glass.

The following morning Margaret did not appear for breakfast. People called for her and searched for her but she could not be found; her bed chamber empty and her sheets unused. The king was distraught and ordered the search to be extended to the castle grounds. Nothing was found save a piece of red material, from one of her dresses, caught on the cliffs beneath the castle. Had she fallen? it was unlikely since she knew these cliffs so well and there was no sign of a body. Perhaps she had been taken by the fairy folk. No one knew, least of all the king, who fell into a state of deep grief.

Then one day, one of the local chieftains came to the castle, asking only for the king.

He bowed low, 'Sire', he said. 'There is a laidly worm on Spindlestone Heugh, causing terror amongst the citizens.'

'A laidly worm, a dragon at Spindlestone Heugh?'

'Yes, sire, its tail is wound around the Bridlestone. Each day it grows another foot, its eyes staring out towards the Farne Islands and roaring as if in great distress.'

'Are you drunk, man?' said the king. 'You'll be strung up, if you are!'

'No sir, the beast is true, any man from Spindlestone will tell you so, and it has a voracious appetite. The only thing that will calm it down is milk. The farmers are pouring seven gallons each day into a stone trough and still the beast grows.'

'What damage is it doing?' said the king incredulous.

'It seems to have no interest in harming folk, apart from the cost of the milk, which is dear, sire.

Only its venomous breath is poisoning and scorching all the pasture for miles around; it will ruin the whole country. Indeed I have little grass left for my cattle. The farmers are in despair.'

'Have you not men that can rid us of this thing?'

'Many men have tried with pitchforks and lances but nothing will enter its scaly skin.'

'I will send soldiers at once.'

'I believe,' said the chieftain, 'that only your son, Childe Wynd, can rid us of this beast.'

'Then I will send messages that he should come at once,' said the king.

Childe Wynd, however, was already on his way across the sea from France, booty filling the coffers of many chests.

The new queen kept her ears close to the ground and when the first sight of sails was seen on the far horizon, she took herself to a place on the windy cliff top. She had no desire to have the king's son meddling into her business. She looked out across the grey, steely ocean and used her power to conjure up a storm. Throwing her arms into the air and shrieking into the waves. And indeed the sea and sky responded; a fierce wind whipped out into the ocean, creating gigantic breakers that pounded on to the rocks and shore. Try as he might, Childe Wynd could not battle through it. The captain of the boat turned to him. 'That is no ordinary storm, there is witchcraft in it. We must return and build a boat of rowan wood.'

So they arrived back in France where men sawed and jointed planks of rowan to create a new boat. It was several months later that the rowan-wood boat hoisted its red sails and left for Budle Bay. Again the witch queen was waiting and again she summoned a storm but even though it was more powerful than the one before, the boat sliced through the waves to reach the shore. 'There is evil in it', shouted the captain as Child Wynd jumped on to the sands of the bay. Ducks and wading birds rose in a frenzy above his head, wheeling around in the wind.

Above, on the rocks of Spindlestone, the laidly worm watched. Then very quietly it slid through gorse and birch, towards the bay. Childe Wynd saw it coming and drew his sword. But the creature made no sign of defence or retreat. It crossed the mud straight towards him, its huge head looking down from a scaly neck.

Chlide Wynd looked up into the beast's eyes and raised his blade. In that instant he noticed something strange. It had eyes the colour of flax blossom that evoked a familiar yearning memory in him. He hesitated. A strange, guttural rumbling noise came from deep in the worm's belly and it spoke:

Quit thy sword and bend thy bow,
And give me kisses three;

If I'm not won ere the sun goes down,
Won I shall never be.*

Despite the fact that the voice was deep, he knew it, though he was not sure from where. Childe Wynd sheathed his sword, leaned forward and to the amazement of all watching, kissed the worm three times on its stinking lips.

Slowly the mighty beast transformed, scales started to fall from its body, its mighty head retracted, its limbs became pale and soft. There before him stood his sister, Margaret, her eyes wild and frightened. Childe Wynd wrapped his red cloak around her naked body.

'Thank you, my brother,' she said softly, 'I knew you must come in time.' Then her voice hardened like steel. 'It is the new queen who did this.'

Together they walked along the soft sand toward Bamburgh Castle and climbed up the cliffs they knew so well.

The queen and king were supping on sweetmeats when the brother and sister entered the dining room. The king's face lit up. The queen's drained of colour; words stumbled out of her mouth.

'Oh, you're back, you must …' She made as if to leave.

'Stay', said Childe Wynd.

'You've done enough damage,' said Margaret. 'It is time for you to receive the blessing of a laidly worm.'

And as the word 'blessing' came from Margaret's lips, the witch queen began to shrivel, her skin becoming wrinkled, warty and brown. Until there, in her place, squatting on the cold palace floor, was a toad.

Childe Wynd flicked it with his foot and out of the window into a flower bed.

And if I'm not mistaken there is a great toad lolloping around the castle grounds to this day.

* Written by Robert Lambert, Vicar of Norham, in 1778, and thought to be taken from a ballad by Duncan Fraser, a Cheviot bard, in 1270. See Henderson, *Notes on the Folklore of the Northern Counties and Borders*.

SIR GUY THE SEEKER

To the south of Bamburgh is Dunstanburgh Castle which sits gaunt and ruined on the edge of precipitous cliffs looking over the grey North Sea. The sky reels with kittiwakes and fulmars whilst the waves pound on the rocks beneath. It must be one of the most dramatic castles in Britain and an obvious site for a story of chivalry and romance. This tale is created from a metrical legend written by Monk Lewis in 1809.

One cold winter's night, Sir Guy was making his way along the coast of Northumberland on horseback. The wind was blowing a gale and the clouds heavy and dark. He was frozen to the bone, weary and in need of shelter. Then through the swirling mist he saw the looming shape of Dunstanburgh Castle. The knight urged his mount forwards until he reached its mighty doors, which were firmly closed. Sir Guy thumped his gloved fist on the wood but it remained solid and unmoving, so he tied his mount to a nearby yew tree and crouched in the porch out of the worst of the weather. But the wind only blew stronger and the waves thundered into the rumble churn in the cliffs below. A streak of lightening lit the dark sky, followed by a crash of thunder that seemed to shake the very foundations of the castle. The waves from the sea exploded into the cliff arcing high above the castle walls. Sir Guy's horse broke its reins and galloped off inland. At that moment the gates opened to reveal a giant of a man, whose shaven head danced with flames and who held in his raised hand a bar of red hot burning iron. He beckoned to Sir Guy saying:

> Sir Knight, Sir Knight!
> If your heart be right,
> And your nerves be firm and true, Sir Knight, Sir Knight!
> A Beauty bright In durance waits for you.

The storm abated and there was an eerie silence as Sir Guy followed the flaming man up a spiral staircase. Round and round they climbed, past dank walls, until they came to the third floor where in front of them was a door with a snake curled around as the latch. The animal hissed and darted its fanged mouth towards Sir Guy before his guide clasped it firmly and swung open the door.

Inside was a marbled room illuminated by a soft blue light whilst all around the walls stood horses and below them sleeping knights.

> And of marble black as the raven's back
> A hundred steeds stood round;
> And of marble white by each a knight
> Lay sleeping on the ground.

In the centre of the room was a crystal tomb guarded on either side by the skeleton of an ancient king, one holding a falchion sword and the other a horn. Sir Guy looked into the crystal coffin and his eyes rested on a woman, more beautiful than any he had ever seen. She lay in complete stillness. He knelt down beside her and tears flowed down his cheeks.

'How might I release you,' he whispered but the maiden did not speak and simply moved her hands together in prayer.

From the corner, Sir Guy heard the words of the flaming man.

'That coffin was made with the devil's hands. No man can open it. To break the spell, you must either blow the horn or draw the sword. That is the riddle you must answer.'

'How do I know which to choose?' he mumbled, expecting no reply – and getting none.

Sir Guy walked to the skeletal king, holding the sword and put his hand on it. Then a voice inside his head said, 'You're wrong, Sir Guy.' He hesitated.

'It must be the horn.'

Sir Guy moved to the other king, grasped the horn and put it to his lips. He blew a strong, shill blast that echoed around the vaulted room. The horses stamped their hooves. The sleeping knights began to rise. They moved towards him with stony eyes. Sir Guy put out his hand to take the sword. But the minute he released the horn, there was a wild cry. Sir Guy's heart rose only to be broken. Everything went dark. There was silence save for the mocking voice of the flaming man.

> Now shame on the coward who sounded a horn,
> When he might have unsheathed a sword!

Sir Guy found himself lying soaked at the castle entrance, the shameful words echoing in his mind.

'I will draw the sword now!' He cried, but search as he might he could not find the winding staircase, the vaulted room or the crystal tomb, where the maiden slept.

For much of his life he wandered the castle looking for a way in. He is long gone now but still remains in ghostly form, searching, searching, searching for the love he might have had.

It is said that some years ago a party of visitors from North Shields came to Dunstanburgh for a sightseeing trip and asked a local lad to take them round. He refused saying he would not go there because of 'him', *the one that wandered around*. One of the party offered him a sixpence, however, and all the lad's fear suddenly evaporated!

The Sleeping King of Sewingshields

In central Northumberland, Hadrian's Wall passes along the Whin Sill, a hard rocky ridge whose origin is the molten magma of the centre of the earth. At a certain places along that ridge ancient stories emerge out of the misshapen rocks. These are stories of hidden things, heroes, strife and treasure. This one is based in an old castle called Sewingshields, which is no longer visible above the ground and has been a ruin for many years. In 1828 the historian Hodgson described it as 'a square, low, lumpy mass overgrown with nettles'.

The shepherd sat on the mound of old Sewingshields, darning his sock. The sheep were settled, the hay was in and he had time on his hands. So he dreamed as he knitted. An insect bit him on the back of his neck and reaching to brush it off, he absent-mindedly dropped his clew. He watched helplessly as the ball of wool rolled down the hill, tumbling its way between the briars and brambles. It was a precious thing, spun by his mother, so he scrambled down after it, surprised that it had not got tangled in the thorns. The shepherd followed the strand until he found himself in a dark place below a ledge but still the line continued. It seemed almost like a living creature leaving a trail. He went where it led him until it disappeared into thick vegetation.

The young man cleared the thorns away until he revealed a secret passageway into which the strand of wool had disappeared. He crouched down and crawled inside until he was in darkness. He could not see but felt fat toads squatting on the damp passage floor, over which he had to carefully manoeuvre his body. Bats flitted past him. It was an unholy place and he hesitated, losing courage, but there in the gloom ahead was a strange, faint light. It lit up the far end of the cavern a luminous green. He continued crawling, keeping his hand on the precious line of wool. The passage suddenly opened into a huge vaulted cavern. In the centre of the floor was a crack in the rock, from which a flame danced, emitting an unearthly glow into the dread silence.

He looked around and found himself in a theatre of thrones and elegant couches on which men lay, attired in the costumes of war but with their chests heaving in deep sleep. At their feet lay sleeping hounds and in the centre of the room a king and queen sat dressed in cloaks of green. They each wore a crown that sparkled with the reflected light of precious jewels of many colours. In front of them was a table covered with a green cloth, on which lay a sword, a garter and a bugle horn.

The shepherd stood very still, looking around to take it all in. He had entered another world which chilled him but he knew the stories and understood what was being asked of him. He trembled and then with slow deliberate footsteps he walked towards the green covered table. He stretched out his arm, picked up the sword and slowly removed it from its sheath. The knights began to twitch, their heads to slowly rise, but the shepherd continued. He brought the blade gently down to cut through the garter. He glanced up, the king's eyes flickered open for a moment. The shepherd re-sheathed the sword. He noticed the enchantment take hold of the knights again, their bodies slumping. But the king stayed upright, his now wide-open eyes looked at the shepherd. His lips moved and he opened his mouth to speak.

Suddenly terror swept through the young man. He lost his nerve, turned and ran, ducking his head and scrabbling into the passage, desperate for the outside world and the light. A deep voice followed him, echoing amongst the rocky fissures.

> Oh woe betide that evil day
> On which this witless wight was born
> Who drew the sword, the garter cut
> But never blew the bugle horn.*

He arrived at his home shaking with fear, spitting out words to his family that they barely understood. The following morning, however, he realised that somehow he had fled from his destiny. He went back to find the wool and the strange entrance into the rock but his memory had completely deserted him and he could find neither the clew nor the passageway.

* Taken from John Hodgson, *A History of Northumberland.*

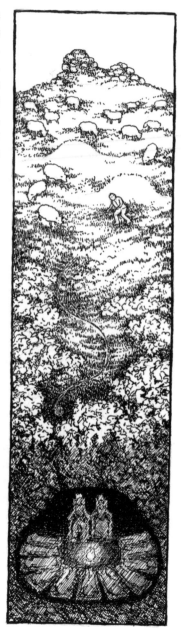

GUINEVERE'S COMB

The Arthur theme continues just a mile or so to the west where there are two rocky outcrops, known as the King's and Queen's Crags. Here Arthur and Guinevere once sat. The story goes that Guinevere once provocatively brushed her dark hair in Arthur's face, which sent him into such a rage that he hurled a rock at her. Guinevere, however, merely batted it to the ground with her comb where the rock now lies, indented with the marks of its teeth.

THE TREASURE OF BROOMLEE LOUGH

Tracing the Whin Sill westwards along the line of Hadrian's Wall you eventually reach Broomlee Lough, hidden from the view of walkers by the folds of the land. It is an extraordinary place that seems to hold the huge sky in its depths, changing constantly from one indefinable shade of silver to the next.

There was a chieftain of old who lived in the border land of Sewingshields Castle, who had amassed a great wealth of gold and silver. He kept it secure in his castle but he was ever fearful of the threats of the marauding Scots from across the border. He held this treasure dearer to him than his own family; much blood had been spilt in its acquisition.

One day his scouts came through the castle gates, breathless. 'There is a great force of men coming from over the hill armed with spears and clubs.' One man shouted. The chief looked out and saw that his troops were defenceless in comparison. His thoughts were only of his treasure. He needed to find somewhere safe to hide it away from enemy hands. He loaded it into a chest and on to a horse-drawn cart and called his sorcerer to him.

The two of them fled to the west, leaving his people to fend for themselves. The dust kicked up by the invading mob was visible on the horizon and they galloped furiously until they reached Broomlee Lough. They untied a small boat and loaded the chest of treasure on to it. The chief and his sorcerer rowed out into the deep centre until they found a place where no man would likely go. Here the chieftain tipped his hoard overboard, watching it sink into the peaty depths. He turned to his sorcerer and instructed him to put a spell on the treasure. The magician stood, rocking in the small boat, and opened his arms, chanting:

> But let it lie till the crack of doom
> In the depths of the Lough of the Ley of Broom
> Unless some man of our kindly race
> Should come to possess this pleasant place,
> And let him then with two twin yauds,
> Two twin oxen and two twin lads,
> And a chain that's been forged by a smith of kind,
> Get it out if he can find.*

What happened to the chieftain and whether he ever returned to attempt to recover his booty we do not know. We do know that the story was told from generation to generation and the spell remembered. Some years later a farmer decided to try his luck finding the treasure for himself. He studied the lines of the spell.

He needed a chain made by a 'smith of kind', which is a blacksmith who is the seventh in an unbroken line of smiths. He needed two yauds (heavy horses) and two lads (young men). He harnessed his two best horses and called on his two eldest sons. Then he waited for a day that was breezy not windy. He untied his boat and rowed out to the place in the centre of the lough where no ripples formed. He dropped the chains into the water and pulled until they snagged on something heavy and then rowed ashore. He tied the end of the chain to the horses and with the help of the lads, they pulled. They could feel the treasure dragging along the bottom of the lough, then it snagged. They redoubled their effort. and just as it started to move again, a link in the chain broke.

* Taken from M.A. Richardson, *A Local Historian's Table Book*.

The treasure was gone and try as they might, they could not find it again.

Story had it that the chain broke because the smith wasn't truly the seventh of an unbroken line. His supposed 'smith' grandfather had been away at Willimoteswick on business for a few days when a travelling man had visited his grandmother in the farm, and nine months later she gave birth.

More recently divers have entered the lough to see if they could find the treasure. But what hope had they without the correct chain?

It is also quite possible that the origins of this story are much older than the one I have written here. The man of 'kindly race' in the spell could refer to one of the Celtic people who lived in the area before the Romans came. The Celts saw the ability of a person to transform rock into metal as magical, so a blacksmith is likely to have a role in a transformative spell. Also, what in the story was seen as material treasure could have been, in the old Celtic mythologies, a spiritual treasure, the entrance to the 'other world', the magical realm of the spirits. So, far from finding some mundane gold and silver under the water, what we, perhaps, should be looking for is the passageway to another dimension.

THE HERMIT OF WARKWORTH

A large swathe of Northumberland is or has been owned by the various earls and dukes of Northumberland. On this land they have built the imposing castles of Alnwick, where Harry Potter was filmed, and Warkworth. This story takes place in the fourteenth century sometime after King Edward III had gifted Warkworth Castle to his trusted ally Lord Percy in order to help secure the border from the Scots.

One of Lord Percy's knights, Lord Bertram, had an eye for the beautiful Isabel, the daughter of Lord Widdrington. One evening, Lord Percy was having one of his regular parties at Alnwick Castle when Lord Bertram found himself face to face with Isabel.

Bertram seized the moment and announced his love for her, asking for her hand in marriage. Lady Isabel was flattered by the proposal but, as was the custom, wasn't going to accept without some display of chivalry on his behalf. So she instructed one of her maids to hand him a steel helmet, which was a code for saying, 'do some daring knightly deed and I'm yours'.

Lord Percy, seeing what was going on, sought to help his friend and announced to the assembled company that he would be taking a party to make a raid on Earl Douglas in the Scottish borders and that Lord Bertram was invited to be amongst them.

Bertram accepted at once, delighted to have a chance to show his honour.

The following day Betram donned his steel helmet and rode with the raiding party up to the Douglas stronghold. Here he entered into the fray with great gusto, thrashing at any one in a kilt he could find. Unfortunately he didn't see one of these skirted warriors come up behind him and bring his axe with full force down on his head. The helmet saved Bertram's life but he was badly wounded and had to be rescued by his companions. They retreated to Wark where they left Bertram to convalesce in relative safety.

For a while it was touch and go as to whether he would live, so the forlorn Bertram sent a message to Isabel to come and see him immediately. He slowly recovered but Isabel never arrived. Confused and dispirited, the remorseful Bertram rode with his brother to Widdrington to find what had happened to his ladylove. On arrival, the lord was surprised to see Bertram without Isabel and told him that she had departed immediately on receiving his message, some weeks before.

Lord Bertram cursed himself for his weakness in expecting her to travel all that way to see him. It was clear what must have happened. Her party would have been waylaid by some marauding Scots en route to Wark. Bertram was beside himself with anxiety and he and his brother agreed to go separate ways to search for her, so they could cover a larger area. For many days Bertram rode back towards the borders, dressed as a peasant to disguise his identity and asking questions as to who might have seen what.

Eventually his path led to the tower at Hethpool in the far north of the Cheviot Hills. It was occupied by a Scottish chieftain, who for a long time had had eyes for Isabel. Bertram arrived there in the evening and hid himself in a clump of bushes some distance away so he could see who was coming and going. He peered as best he could into the tower windows and imagined for a moment he had caught sight of his loved one.

Soon he drifted off to sleep. He was woken in the morning by a muffled cry coming from the direction of the tower and there he saw Isabel lying on the ground at the base of the wall with a man wearing a Scottish bonnet standing over her. In a rage Bertram raced over to save her, drawing his sword as he did so. Without a second thought he brought the blade swinging down towards the neck of her captor but as he did so, Isabel leapt between them crying, 'Stop, it's your brother.' But the movement of the sword was unstoppable. It slashed into Isabel's breast and on to the throat of his brother. The two of them fell to the ground with that single blow.

Bertram knelt down and cradled their heads in his hands but it was too late, they were both mortally wounded and died in his arms. He had managed to kill his two most precious companions with one stroke of blind fury.

Bertram entered into a great despair and eventually returned to Warkworth, where he gave away all his money and possessions to the poor. He asked permission to build a hermitage on the bank of the river. This he did, with his own hands, and spent the rest of his life there in prayer.

There is an inscription above the doorway in Latin, which if translated reads:

Tears have been my meat night and day.

The hermitage sits beneath Warkworth Castle to this day.

THE JINGLING MAN

There was once a cave in the cliff beneath Tynemouth Castle. It has now been blocked up and there is only a narrow slit where the entrance once was. You can shine a torch beam in a little way but what now lies beyond is anyone's guess.

There is a cave in the rocks just beneath Tynemouth Castle where a pirate known as Jingling Geordie once lived. This pirate used to lure ships by placing lanterns on the rocks of the Black Middens at the mouth of the Tyne. Sailors would be confused into thinking they were boats in harbour and would sail towards them, only to run aground in the treacherous waters. These sailors would abandon their vessels and struggle ashore for safety and to get help. As soon as they were out of the way, the pirate would crawl out of his hole in the rocks and help himself to whatever booty was on board before anyone else got there.

Geordie jingled whenever he moved for he wore fetters around his ankles and wrists from a time when he had been chained up for a felony he had committed on the high seas. He held bitterness in his heart and had little mercy for anyone. Jingling Geordie didn't move far from his cave, rarely leaving the rocks of the seashore. He gathered driftwood and on a small fire would boil up limpets, whelks and razor-shells, which he collected from the rocks. These he would eat, together with dried seaweed and whatever he managed to scrounge from the galleys of the wrecks.

Deep in the dark recesses of his cave Jingling Geordie stashed his considerable wealth. Piles of gold, silver and glittering jewels robbed from the ships. People told stories of his riches but few ever dared venture inside the cave for there were other creatures there too. The back of Geordie's cave plunged deep into the earth, down to where the creatures of the underworld live. The eight-legged ones, the slimy ones, the dragons; they were all there and at first they resented the pirate occupying the entrance to their cave. That is until they saw the hoard of treasure that he had accumulated.

The truth is that there is nothing a dragon likes more than a hoard of treasure. So Jingling Geordie struck a deal. The dragons would protect him and in return they got to curl their tails around his glittering piles of gold and silver. It was an amicable enough arrangement and perhaps that is why Geordie was never seen splashing his fortune in the clubs and bars of Whitley Bay.

It seems that the dragons survived long after Jingling Geordie had gone. For there was a knight called Walter, born in Whitley Bay, who, as a child, had been told stories by his mother of the fabulous treasures inside the cave below the castle on the Tynemouth cliffs. It was his favourite story and once, curled up on his mother's lap, he had made a secret promise to himself that one day he would be the one to find that treasure. It was in the early years of his knighthood that he remembered that promise. Others had tried and failed but Walter believed that it was his destiny to honour that childhood dream.

It was on midsummer's day, the eve St John, his patron saint, that Walter set out. The sun glittered over the sea as he followed the path down the cliffs exactly as he remembered from the story. The cliffs were steep and slimy and difficult to climb, but he eventually levered himself into the entrance to the hole, his armour shining and his hand on his sword.

He had not expected what he encountered there. The clamour, the sounds and the stench of the creatures of the underworld turned his stomach as much as his heart. But his dream held him fast and he sliced through the slippery ones, the slimy ones and the ones with many arms. He advanced deeper and deeper into the dark depths of the cave. Spectres shrieked and pulled him in many directions to distract him from his mission, but his heart was true and eventually he came to a mighty door over which hung a bugle. Walter reached up but as soon as he touched it, the horn became a snake writhing in his hand. He put his lips to the mouthpiece, which became the snake's open jaw but he held fast and blew once, twice, three times. The door opened to reveal a large and brightly lit hall supported by columns of jasper and crystal; shimmering lamps illuminated piles of gold and glittering gems.

Around the hoard curled the tail of a mighty dragon. The beast raised its head and looked at Walter the Bold with one eye open. As Walter raised his sword, he heard a mighty rumble issue from the dragon's stomach, hot breath stream from its nostrils, its claws scratch the ground, its eyes glare bright and fierce. His instinct was to flee: he was no match for this monster. It was then Walter the Bold remembered the song his mother had sung to him to send him to sleep at the end of this very story. He sheathed his sword and sang as he walked around the mighty beast. Its body slowly drooped and it slumbered. Walter gathered gems and made a pile of the treasure outside of the sleeping beast's tail. Some things he touched came easily, others caused that same rumble in the dragon's belly and those he left.

Walter the Bold left that hole in Tynemouth's cliff with enough treasure to buy a hundred castles, and thus he became known as the Lord of a Hundred Castles. But he also built a monastery to honour his good fortune and was generous with what he had, saying that it was all because of a song and a slumbering dragon.

> Gold heaped upon gold, and emeralds green
> And diamonds and rubies, and sapphires untold
> Rewarded the courage of Walter the Bold.*

* Taken from William Hone, *The Year Book of Daily Recreation and Information*.

6

BETWEEN WORLDS

TAM LIN

Tam Lin is best known as a border ballad and is a story that straddles the borders both between different countries and different worlds of the imagination. It is commonly associated with Carterhaugh in Selkirkshire, Scotland, though it may come from Carter Bar on the English side of the border in Northumberland. So the geography, like the story itself, is a place of uncertainty.

It was midsummer. Janet tucked her green dress up above her knee, tied back her yellow hair and walked out of her father's substantial house. She stepped lightly towards the woods, intoxicated by the smells and sounds of this, the longest day of the year. She soon entered into the shaded world of mighty oaks and elms, and picked her way along small paths and by rushing burns until she came to a well. There she saw a beautiful wild rose and, fancying it to decorate her hair, she plucked two flowers.

A man's voice broke her revelry. 'How dare you pick those roses without my permission?' It said. She looked up and there he stood amongst the trees on the other side of the well.

'I can take what I like, my father gave this wood to me and I'll not ask your permission to come here.' As she spoke the young man simply smiled and looked at her with his deep eyes. She was also conscious of being overwhelmed by a musty fragrance. She remembered little else of that afternoon, except the softness of the grass and the gentleness of his arm.

When she arrived back at her father's house she knew she was carrying his child.

Slowly her belly grew and the garments she wore could hide her coming maternity no longer. Her father questioned her. 'Which squire is responsible for this?'

'It has nothing to do with your squires.' She told her father, 'I have only myself to blame for I believe the child belongs to an elf. And the truth is that I would not change his love for that of one of your earthly knights.'

It was not until the end of October – Samhain – that she was drawn to the wood again. Was she seeking rue or some other herb to flush the growing babe from her body? Possibly, she wasn't sure – but more likely she went because the place pulled her there. Amongst the yellowing leaves of oak and elm, she saw him standing by the spring, a milk white steed by his side.

'I don't even know your name,' she said.

'My Name is Tam Lin,' he replied.

'Why do you dwell in this place?'

'I have no choice,' he answered,' I am held here.'

'What holds you?' she asked.

He smiled once more, 'I was returning from hunting with my grandfather one cold day when I fell from my horse. I do not know what tugged me from my mount. Perhaps it was the hand of the fairy queen. All I know is that I awoke under that green mound and found myself trapped in fairy land.'

Tam Lin pointed to a clearing in the forest. 'It is pleasant enough as time does not pass as it does in the mortal world, but …' He shuddered and stopped talking.

'What is it you fear?' said Janet.

'Every seven years, the fairy queen has to pay a tithe to hell; the time is soon and I fear it will be me for I am fair in looks and fit and strong.'

'What can I do to help free you from this place?' She asked as her hands stroked the child in her belly.

'There is one chance,' said Tam Lin. 'On Samhain, at the stroke of midnight, the fairies ride upon the earth. If one has a true love, she must wait at mile cross.'

'How will I know you and what I should do?' said Janet.

'First you will see the black horses, then you will see the brown, after that will come a milk-white steed and that one is mine. I will have one gloved hand and one bare. A cocked hat and combed down hair. You must pull me from the horse and wrestle me to the ground, then hold me as tight as you can. I will change from a man to a snake, from a snake to a lion, from a lion to a glowing bar of iron and lastly to a red hot coal. Throw the coal into the well. Then find me as a naked man and wrap me in your cloak. Remember, I will not harm you if you hold me tight and I will return to be the father of your child.' Tam Lin's words came to an end and he left without another word.

It was a murky night as Janet waited at mile cross, and at the stroke of midnight she heard the tinkling of bridles. She watched and from the undergrowth they appeared. First the black horse came bearing the fairy queen, followed by the brown one and then the milk white steed, bearing Tam Lin with one hand gloved and the other not.

Janet leapt and pulled her lover from the saddle. Immediately she found herself holding a slithery, slippery snake that wound around her body; then the claws and teeth of a wild lion that ripped and pulled at her flesh; then the red hot iron that transformed into a glowing coal and burnt her hands. Was it the power of the child in her belly that enabled her to throw the coal into the well? But throw it she did and there she found her naked man, whom she wrapped in her protective cloak.

The queen of the fairies turned and scowled.

'Had I known that my finest, fairy knight was in league with a mortal like you, I would have replaced your fair eyes with wood.' She said bitterly.

But the truth was it was too late for the fairy queen. Tam Lin had crossed the veil between worlds and rejoined that of the mortals.

Janet led him home and what came of them after that we do not know.

Childe Rowland

In this story the lower reaches of the River Tweed mark the border between the two nations of Scotland and England, whilst the waves of the North Sea lap the sands of the Northumberland coast. Joyous Gard of legend may well have been Bamburgh Castle.

On the north bank of the Tweed there lived a queen with three sons and a daughter. The daughter was called Burde Ellen and the youngest son was called Childe Rowland.

One midsummer day, the boys were playing with a ball in the church graveyard when the eldest kicked it so high that it landed on the other side of the church. He shouted to his sister to hurry up and bring him back his ball. Now, Burde Helen, wanting to please her eldest brother, ran around the church to collect it. But she was not thinking and she ran widdershins and did not come back.

The boys looked for her and called her name, 'BURDE ELLEN, BURDE ELLEN', but she was nowhere to be seen and they went to tell their mother.

'Which way around the church did she run?' said the queen. 'Widdershins', said the elder boy.

'Widdershins, on Midsummer Day!' cried the queen. 'She should have gone sun-wise, that is very foolish. The fairies will have taken her.'

The eldest brother drew himself to his full stature and said, 'Tell me how to find her and I will bring her back.'

'Only the wizard Merlin can tell you that,' the queen replied. 'To find him you must travel across the borderland to the castle of Joyous Gard, where Merlin is staying with Sir Lancelot.

For the eldest brother this was a good excuse to put on his shining armour and don his plumed helmet. 'Saddle my bay horse,' he ordered Childe Rowland, as he got himself ready for his journey. He rode off to the south and crossed the River Tweed into the border lands of Northumberland. Then he galloped, with the sea to his left, until he came to the mighty castle of Bamburgh. He shuddered when he looked up at the towering walls but rode onwards until he met a knave who led him beyond the mighty doors, through long dark corridors to a vaulted room. There he found himself kneeling at the feet of Merlin.

'Widdershins!' exclaimed Merlin, 'on Midsummer's Day!' 'She will be captured by the King of Fairyland and taken for his wife. It will take great courage to bring her back but there is a chance if you listen very carefully to my instructions.'

Merlin spoke clear words from his aging lips. But the elder brother only half heard what the magician said. His mind was too preoccupied with imagining the glory of his heroic return, his younger sister by his side.

After several months the elder brother had not returned to his family. The middle brother came to his mother, the queen, 'My brother has not come back, let me go and rescue my sister.' She nodded sadly and he too left with his shining armour, his plumed helmet and his fine stallion. They waited and waited but he never came back.

'I will go,' said Childe Rowland. But his mother refused. 'You are my one remaining child,' she pleaded. 'What will be the future, if you too do not return?'

'Let me go,' said the boy 'and I shall come back with my sister and my two brothers.'

She sighed and let him go. Their wealth was spent; he had no Barbary bay, no shining armour and no plumed helmet. He had an old horse and ordinary clothes but his mother turned to him and said: 'Childe Rowland, take this,' and lifted from the wall the claymore, that had belonged to his father. 'It has never been struck in vain,' she said. 'Use it well!'

Childe Rowland rode slowly to the bank of the Tweed, looking for the shallowest place for his steed to cross, and then rode into Northumberland. For many miles he journeyed with the pounding sea to his left, past the holy Island of Lindisfarne, the Spindlestone Crags and on to the mighty doors of Bamburgh Castle.

Merlin nodded as he entered the room with the vaulted ceiling. 'I hope your ears are less confused than those of your brothers,' he said. Childe Rowland simply bowed to the great man. 'To retrieve

your sister, you must listen well and have great faith and courage.'
Merlin paused and looked directly into Childe Rowland's eyes. 'You
must travel north and west until the sun has sunk low over the land
and the shadows are long. There you will see a round hill and at its
foot a rowan tree with early red berries. When you pass this you have
entered fairyland. You must use your father's sword to remove the
head of any person who speaks to you. Walk three times widdershins
around the hill and shout 'open'. You can then enter into the king's
palace but whatever you do, no matter how hungry or thirsty, you
must neither eat nor drink or you will fall asleep.'

Merlin took the Claymore from Chile Rowland and spoke some words across it, 'The King of Fairyland will have magic, but this will match it blow for blow.'

Childe Rowland mounted his horse and was surprised by its youthful vigour as he rode. The shadows were long when he reached a rowan tree with bright red berries. He dismounted his horse and tethered it. Behind was a rounded hill, around which he started to walk widdershins but before he had gone around once, he saw a cowherd. 'Which is the way to the king's palace?' he asked, 'you must ask the swineherd up ahead,' the cowherd replied. Childe Rowland swung the sword, which had never been used in vain, and hewed off the cowherd's head. Before he had walked around a second time he came to the swineherd.

'Which is the way to the king's palace?' he asked.

'You must ask the henwife,' replied the swineherd. Childe Rowland swung the sword, which had never been used in vain, and took off his head too. Before he had completed the third round he saw the henwife.

'You look tired,' said the henwife sweetly, 'why don't you come inside and rest with a cup of tea?' Childe Rowland was tempted but then he remembered Merlin's words and swung the sword for a third time, which took off her head also. He heard something chuckle and scamper away.

The top of the hill was terraced, circular marks decorated the ground. 'Open', he cried and from one of the marks a door appeared that opened into the centre of the hill.

Childe Rowland ducked into a rough hewn passageway, which, though devoid of sunlight, shone with the soft radiance of shimmering silver and spar, encrusted on translucent walls. He made his way carefully down the passage until he entered a chamber, filling almost the entire length and breadth of the hill. Here, hanging from the ceiling, was a huge pearl rotating slowly and radiating a warm glow, like the setting sun. At the far end was his sister, Burd Ellen seated on a golden sofa, a soft smile on her lips and their two sleeping brothers at her feet. He wanted to run, shout and hold her in his arms but something about the place stopped him. The silks, satins and soft carpets, filling the room, created a deadly hush. Instead he tiptoed noiselessly and crouched at her feet. He whispered to her but it seemed she was not there. Then overcome with a mighty tiredness and hunger he said, 'Will you not at least offer your brother food and drink after his long journey?'

He saw her wince but she said nothing and rose to fetch him a silver goblet of milk and a plate of warm bread. He raised the food to his lips but again remembering Merlin's words, he pushed them back to her saying, 'I will neither taste nor touch until I have set you free'. No sooner were the words out of his mouth than the hall doors were flung open and in strode the King of Fairyland.

'What human had dared set foot in the dark tower of Elfland?' he roared.

Fi fi fo and fum!
I smell the blood of a Christian man!
Be he dead or be he living, wi my brand
I'll clash his brains frea his brain-pan!*

For a moment the two men stared at each other and then Childe Rowland drew his claymore. 'Strike, if you dare. I come to take my sister and two brothers back to their land.'

'Ha!' retorted the king, 'If you are as fickle as those two, you may as well lay your arms down now!'

They both swung their swords and the sound of the clashing steel echoed through the chamber. But Childe Rowland was not as fickle as his brothers, and just as the magician Merlin prophesied, his claymore matched the sword of the King of the Fairies blow for blow. Childe Rowland was the younger and lither and eventually he had the king pinned to the ground.

'Restore them and let them free, and I'll do you no harm.'

'You have an awesome magic, it can only be the work of Merlin. Let me up.' said the fairy king. The defeated king went from the room and returned with a phial of bright red liquid. He let fall a

* Taken from Joseph Jacobs, *More English Fairy Tales.*

tiny droplet on to each of the brother's nostrils, eyes and mouth. Their sleep was lifted and they rose.

The king bowed to Burde Helen, carefully applied the droplets of red liquid to her eyes and said: 'You, whom I was to have as my wife, I release you from the enchantment.' Two tears ran down her cheeks and she too rose.

Burde Ellen embraced her brothers and the three of them walked out into the starry night without looking back.

In an instant, the whole of fairy world was gone from their memories and they meandered their way home.

The Faa's Revenge

In the North of the Cheviot Hills lies the border town of Kirk Yetholm, at the end of the Pennine Way. If you go into the Border Inn you will see, on the walls, photographs of the King of the Gypsies, William Faa. In times past this was the stronghold of the northern gypsies, who took their clan name from their leader. Further south in the eastern foothills of the Cheviots is Clennell Hall, a large manor house adjacent to Clennell Street, an ancient drove road. This track heads north all the way to the Scottish borders, making travel between the two places not so difficult.

It was a bitterly cold night when Andrew Smith, head of the domestics at the Clennell Manor, was doing a final check before retiring to bed for the night. He opened the door of one of the outbuildings, thrust his lamp inside and saw a group of poorly dressed people crouched over a little fire.

'Out!' he said in the most authoritative voice he could muster. 'Get out now.' But none of them stirred. Then a deep voice rumbled from the back, 'Leave us be, we will do no harm and be gone by the morning.' There, standing in the shadows, was the tall, broad-shouldered and unmistakable form of William Faa, king of the gypsies.

Andrew protested. 'If Lord Clennell finds a thing missing we'll both be strung up.'

William Faa, laughed. 'We'll be no trouble and take neither two-footed nor four-footed beast.'

Then his wife, Elspeth Faa, spoke up saying, 'Don't fear for I will put a spell on your lordship so that he will sleep till sunrise.' And with that she made an incantation of words to the fairy folk, which chilled Andrew's bones, but also slightly reassured him.

> Bonny Queen Mab, bonny Queen Mab,
> Wave ye your wee bits o' poppy wings
> Ower Clennel's laird, that he may sleep
> Till I hae washed where Darden springs warmer.*

William Faa spoke again: 'This is hardly the place for a king to pass the night, lead us my good sir to a warmer situation, where our bones may defrost a little.'

'It is not for me to invite you in,' said Andrew. But by now the household servants were gathering around the gypsies, holding out their palms to Elspeth who was reading the lines and telling them of future husbands and lovers.

Elspeth raised her head, 'Look,' she said, 'the light is out in his bedchamber, your lord already sleeps.'

With great anxiety Andrew found himself taking the gypsy crew into the main hall, where fresh logs were put on the fire.

William Faa spoke again, 'Our outsides are warm but our insides are cold, bring us some vitals to fill our bellies.' Andrew offered him cold ham and beer from the servant's larder but Faa protested. 'You offer meagre fare, such as this to a king? Bring hot food and a jug from the larder of my equal.'

Now trapped, in what felt like a snare of his own making, Andrew tiptoed down to the lord's cellar and brought back a large jug of ale and hot mutton. Elspeth, meanwhile, filled her spacious bag with coins and lockets from the gathering domestics, whom she in turn filled with visions of sweet nights with young handsome gentlemen.

* Taken from 'The Faa's Revenge' in John Mackay Wilson, *Tales of the Borders and of Scotland*.

Curiosity overcame Andrew Smith and he found himself holding out a hand to the rotund, dark-skinned gypsy woman. 'It is difficult to read, this one,' she said. 'That timepiece in your jacket pocket should help me see.'

Andrew found himself divesting of more and more valuables, when suddenly the loud voice of his master thundered through the hall.

'What in the name of the Lord is going on here? Get out, the whole thieving lot of you!' he shouted and brought the back of his hand down on Andrew's face, who sprawled across the floor, whimpering and shaking with fear.

'How dare you call us thieving,' said William Faa. 'Was it not your ancestors who came over with the Normans, stealing land from the people and taxing their livestock!'

'You impertinent fellow,' said Clennell. 'Remove yourself and your filthy clan now!'

'So you will send us out on a freezing night like this?' said William Faa.

'Out now and not a word more from you or I'll set the hounds on you.' Clennell shouted back.

The gypsy crew got up and dragged themselves down the passageway but as they left Elspeth turned around and spat out the words. 'You'll rue the day you sent the King of the Gypsies into a night so cold that even the crows shiver on their boughs.'

And rue the day he did, for not long after that, his cattle became sickly, his poultry killed and his corn filched. Lord Clennell nodded, muttering, 'They'll not get away with this as long as I live.' He took a group of thirty men armed with muskets and brands to the gypsy encampment at Kirk Yetholm. William Faa and his men were away. 'No doubt thieving,' said Clennell, with vicious satisfaction. He ordered his men to put brands to each and every-one of the poor dwellings, kicking out at the remaining occupants as they struggled to evade the flames. Then he and his men circled around on their horses watching and laughing as the dwellings went ablaze.

When Faa returned and saw the desolation of his home he swore vengeance. 'We will go this very night and burn their barns, slaughter each and every one of their kye.' But Elspeth held his hand and said 'wait'. 'We can do more damage than that. Clennell and his wife have a child, a small boy who is the apple of their eyes. They would miss him sorely, if anything were to happen to him.' William smiled and nodded.

A few months later, when the boy was playing outside in the gardens of the hall, William Faa, who was hiding amongst the juniper bushes, jumped out and seized him. He ran, with the screaming child in his arms, toward the boundary burn and leapt to the other side. Andrew Wilson, who had witnessed the whole thing, set off in pursuit. He came to the burn and was looking for a place to jump when Faa held out the child over the torrent and said 'Jump and I'll throw the bairn in.'

Andrew was beaten and returned to the hall with the news. Clennell, in a wild fury, gathered his men and rode out to Kirk Yetholm, meaning this time to slaughter the lot. But when he arrived he found that each and every gypsy had gone; search as they might Clennell and his followers could not find them. A great despair descended on Clennell Hall.

Then, some years later, when the pain was beginning to soften, a second blow struck. The Clennells had since had a daughter and had hired a young local woman called Susan to look after her. One afternoon the two of them were out in the gardens at play when they were called in for lunch. There was no reply. Servants were sent out to look for them, and they were met with silence. A search party scoured the estate but maid and daughter had disappeared into thin air.

'The Faas!' said Clennell, but search as he might, they could not be found. Despair became a dark void that seeped into the very fabric of the Clennell household. William Faa's revenge was complete.

It was some years later, when he was out with a hunting party, that Clennell stumbled upon the encampment in a remote, hidden valley. Recognising it at once as being a place of the gypsies, Clennell's fury erupted and he ordered his hounds on them. He charged in, musket in hand and hatred in his heart. The gypsies fled, slashing out with their knives at the dogs as they went. Clennell found one of his hounds snarling at a small girl and a young woman, trying to tear them apart. 'Take the brute off my bairn, you'll have her killed,' she wailed. Clennell ordered the hound to stop, looked up and found he was staring at none other than his old maid Susan. 'Where's my daughter?' he said coldly. Susan's head just nodded downwards and Clennell realised that the little pale skinned girl she'd been trying to protect was his own child. He took her into his trembling arms and kissed her wounds.

Susan accompanied Clennell back to the Hall and used her considerable skills with herbs to help restore the child to health. She explained that she had been desperate for money and hired by the gypsies to infiltrate the household and do the deed; not an uncommon occurrence in those days. She had no idea where the son was, it was a closely guarded secret between King Willie and Elspeth, who had since separated.

But this story had one more unfolding. For one day, Clennell was riding home through the Harbottle woods, when an old man and a boy stopped him in his tracks. Clennell scoffed, grabbing the hilt of his sword. 'I'll not be waylaid by a child,' he said.

'A child indeed,' replied the young man, drawing on his own sword and the two set about combat. Clennell was surprised: this lad had equal skills in swordsmanship to himself and more dexterity. Eventually the youth flicked Clennell's sword from his hand and pinned him to a tree. Clennell was blindfolded and taken on a long journey, far into the woods, where his blindfold was removed. He found himself in a Gypsy camp, standing face to face with William Faa.

Faa looked at the youth and said, 'You shall execute him tomorrow.'

A great crowd assembled the following morning to watch the execution. Clennell had his hands tied to a tree and the young man raised his musket. He was about to pull the trigger when a voice shouted from the crowd.

'Stop! You want to murder your own father?' Everyone turned to see Elspeth standing at the back of the crowd. Her words carried more power than the king and the lad lowered the gun.

'Let there be an end to this hatred,' the old woman said. 'Take your son, Lord Clennell, and mind you give us folk a little more due.'

Clennell lowered his head and rode back to Clennell Hall, his uncertain son at his side.

The Coquet Drainer

This is a curious tale, recorded in the Dictionary of British Folk-Tales *by Katherine Briggs, which may have its origin in a local legend. It all happens in the valley of the River Coquet, which rises high up in the Southern Cheviots Hills. It has its source at Thirl Moor and Yearning Law and then flows through some of the wildest and most beautiful countryside in England, passing by the town of Rothbury to the coast at Amble.*

There was a man who lived with his small daughter and housekeeper on an estate in the upper reaches of the Coquet. Never mind that he had a mansion and had inherited a small fortune, his days looked inwards rather than out. He spent his time in dark rooms drinking and gambling his wealth away rather than caring for his family or land. It had come to a situation that his debts had mounted so high that he feared he would no longer be able to pay for the services of his housekeeper.

Quite different from him was his brother – a generous, open man, who had left the dampness of Northumberland for warmer climes for the sake of his and his wife's health.

One day the gambler received a letter from this brother, which made his heart quicken.

His brother asked him if he would be so good as to take care of his baby son due to the death of his own wife in childbirth, his declining health and poor prospects for recovery. But the phrase that lit up the gambler's eyes was written thus:

I will provide my child with enough wealth to keep him well and
have written a clause in my will, saying that should anything befall
him, his inheritance will pass on to you my dear brother.
Your affectionate brother …

The gambler, of course, replied that he would do anything to help out his brother in this time of crisis and that the child would be a welcome companion for his own daughter. It was all arranged and the baby boy came to live in the mansion house in the Coquet valley, where the brother put him under the care of his loyal housekeeper.

The gambler had little to do with the children; instead, his lifestyle became more and more profligate and he started to get himself into a lot of bother. His fortune ran through his fingers like sand and his debts mounted until he became desperate. The child's inheritance was the only way out. But to get hold of that, the child would have to be 'out of the picture'.

In those days there was a community of gypsies that lived in Kirk Yetholm and they often went from house to house looking for odd jobs and bits of work. They could turn their hands to most things. It was on a blustery winter's afternoon that a Yetholm man turned up at the Coquet mansion.

The master invited the fellow into the house.

'I've got some unusual work for you and I want no questions asked and no word being spread,' he said. The gypsy smiled and nodded. It sounded lucrative.

The man felt in his pocket and pulled out a wad of notes.

'This is to dispose of the child.' He then took out another wad and added, 'This is for your silence!'

The gypsy hesitated and then he put his hand out. How could he refuse such wealth? There was hunger in his community and he had a large number of mouths to feed. 'What do you want me to do?'

'Wait outside,' said the man.

He then shouted to his housekeeper: 'Dress the boy and bring him down the stairs. I am taking him to stay with a friend for a while.'

She intuitively did not trust her master, and as she dressed the boy for his journey, she hung a locket around his neck containing a photograph of his mother and father. She carefully concealed it beneath his clothes.

She delivered the child to her master. 'Here he is, sir; I hope you both have a safe journey.'

The master went outside and thrust the child into the gypsy's arms. 'Drown it,' he said. 'It'll never be found in one of those black pools on the moor, now be off with you.'

It was already late in the afternoon and there was a chill in the air. The gypsy felt the warmth of the baby's body against his. He walked until he found himself high up, squatting and looking into the dark, cold, peaty depths of a mire. He took the child out from under his coat and for the first time looked at it. It stared back, trusting. He thought of his own children and he knew he couldn't do it. He also knew that he couldn't take it back to his family in Yetholm. There were already too many mouths to feed.

Just then he heard a voice. He looked up and above him stood a man with peaty overalls and a spade. The gypsy recognised him instantly as a drainer – one who cuts ditches to drain the land for the sheep to graze.

'Trouble?' said the drainer.

'I can't leave it and I can't take it,' he replied.

The drainer guessed what he was talking about; a hundred scenarios flashed through his mind. But he leant on his spade and said nothing.

'Here, have it,' said the Yetholm man and thrust the baby into the arms of the drainer. He felt in his pocket and took out a wad of notes. 'This should help.' And without another word he walked away.

Now the drainer lived alone in a small thatched cottage. He cooked his own meals and darned his own socks. His company were the peewit, the snipe and the stonechat and in the winter, they were no company at all. He had got used to it, even enjoyed it in a way. There was no point in pining for what you hadn't got and had very little chance of getting.

He watched the Yetholm man stride off into the Cheviot Hills but made no attempt to call him back. It would be difficult, no question about that ... but by God he would look after the child and teach him all he knew about the moors. He felt inside the child's clothing and found the golden locket, there staring at him was a picture of a well-to-do man and woman smiling at the camera. He wondered and nodded: in a small place like this it wouldn't be difficult to find out who they were. Perhaps he would return the boy one day. Whatever happened this was not going to be the upbringing this child was expecting!

The drainer walked back to his cottage and made a small bed in the corner of his room. He ordered regular milk from the local shepherd, who raised an eyebrow but said nothing. He dug ditches with the boy on his back or asleep in the heather. He never tried to find his parents and instead saw him as a gift. The child grew up knowing only this man of the moors as his father. In time he began to help him with his work and the drainer could dig his ditches three times as fast as ever before. He taught his child the call of the golden plover and how to poach a fine salmon from the river.

The young man grew up, until his teenage years were nearly over, and then one day he was out fishing when he heard a fall of rocks and a scream from the other side of a hill. He ran over and there was a young woman sliding perilously toward the edge of a crag. He scrambled down, caught her hand and gently pulled her to safety.

'Thank you,' she said. 'I don't go out so much; I'm not used to the crags. Please come home with me and my father will reward you handsomely.'

The young man shook his head. 'I want no reward, this is my home.' They smiled at each other and shyly went their separate ways.

As is the way of these things, they did meet again. It was summer. He was fishing and she was taking a solitary bathe in a quiet stretch of the river. This time they did talk and discovered that they were both only children and lived not far apart. They met again and it was not long before love blossomed between them. He asked her to marry him and she did not refuse.

'We must go and meet my father,' she said, and that afternoon they sauntered easily down to the big house.

'You'll not marry that wretch!' boomed her father. 'He's nothing but the son of a drainer.'

Plead as the girl might, her father would not budge and banned them from ever meeting again. But the moor had brought them together and was not easily going to let them part.

The lad walked back to his small hut amongst the heather with leaden steps.

'What is it?' said his father. 'I see you are melancholy. Is it to do with your sweetheart?'

The boy looked surprised. He had never told his father.

'How would I not know,' the father said. 'You have been like a lark on the fells these last few months.'

'I am banned from marrying her. She is from a wealthy family. I am just the son of a poor drainer.'

'And where is her house?' said his father. The boy nodded across to the valley where the mansion stood.

His father looked at him. 'I'll tell you one thing that you must never forget, we may be poor country folk but we are the equal of those that live in mansions. There is also something about your birth it is time for me to tell you.'

As they walked together down towards that mansion, the drainer told his son the story of his origins for the first time.

The housekeeper answered the door. 'Please tell your master I have some important business to settle with him,' said the drainer.

She disappeared into the drawing room.

A voice shouted, 'I'll not be entertaining some wretch from the hills, begging for his son.'

'You will,' said the drainer as he stepped through the door. 'For this boy is of your own flesh and blood, that you would have had drowned had I not intervened!'

He produced the gold locket he had found around the baby's neck. The housekeeper started, 'I wondered – such a gentle boy, like his poor father!' She crossed the room and hugged the young man. 'I can vouch for the truth of this: I used to cradle this bairn in my arms.'

The drainer, now speaking with an authority neither he nor his son had ever heard before said. 'You will not only agree to your daughter's marriage to this lad, but you will return his fortune and since, like as not, you have precious little of that left, you will bequeath them this house. If not, I will turn you over to the police for attempted murder.'

'I will stand as witness to that,' said the housekeeper; she too, finding her voice at last after years of silence.

The gambler began to protest but then looked at the resolute faces in front of him and knew his time was up.

So it was that the drainer spent the remainder of his life in a comfortable mansion, with his almost son and his son's wife. The housekeeper stayed too of course and perhaps there is a story there! I do know that the drainer took her up on to the high fells to hear the tinkling song of the laverock (skylark) and the thrumming of the snipe.

HALF OF NORTHUMBERLAND

This story originates from a ballad of many versions. Quite where in Northumberland it is from is unclear. There are over seventy castles, more than in any other English county.

Lord Bateman was rich. He owned grand houses and castles and half of Northumberland into the bargain. He also had a free spirit and was fond of travel, so one day he set off for foreign parts to see what he would find. He sailed east and he sailed south and eventually arrived on the shores of Turkey. He flung himself whole-heartedly into his adventures, but in this land he found a little more than he bargained for. His ways did not quite meet with theirs. They demanded that he bend his knee to their god but Bateman refused.

This angered the locals and he was captured by a Turk who made him haul carts skewered to his naked shoulders. He laboured through narrow alleys and over rough fields until he was so weak he could hardly walk.

For his endeavours, Bateman was rewarded with a dark prison cell, where he was chained to a mighty log and could neither see nor move. He came close to starvation, but not quite broken, he sang of his beloved Northumberland through the bars of his cell:

My hounds they all go masterless,
  My hawks they flee frae tree to tree,
  My youngest brother will heir my lands
  My Northumberland, I'll never see.*

* Taken from Francis James Child, *The English and Scottish Popular Ballads*.

Now the Turk had one daughter called Sushy Pye, who would take the air, walking past the building where Bateman was incarcerated. One day she heard Bateman's sad song issuing from his prison cell. Her heart went out to the singer, and she became intrigued to discover who he was and what he might offer for a helping hand.

She moved close to the walls so her face came near to the source of the song.

'Is it true,' she whispered through the bars. 'That you own much land?'

'I own half of Northumberland and castles and halls besides,' he replied.

'And how much would you give to the lady love that set you free?'

'I would give all of it,' he said, 'to the one that sets me free.'

Sushy Pye went away and crept into her father's bedroom where she lifted his silken pillow. Underneath she found the key to the jail and much money as well.

She bribed the jailer with enough gold to keep him sweet, lit a candle and made her way down the dank passage to the door of Bateman's cell. She took the heavy key and unlocked it.

The man she saw inside was gaunt and thin with tangled hair and ragged clothes. He was barely able to raise himself from the ground. She put out her hand and helped him stand. In the light of the flame, she saw his face light up with such grace and gratitude that she almost loved him.

Sushy Pye took the ragged man to her father's cellar where they ate cake and drank fine wine. She smiled at him and with each glass said: 'To Northumberland, may you be mine.'

'I will make a vow,' she said. 'If in seven years you marry no other woman, then I too will marry no other man.'

She took a gold ring from her finger and broke it in half, keeping one half for herself and giving the other to him. That evening in the gloaming, she took Batemen to the harbour where there were many tall ships, one of which was owned by her wealthy father.

She went to each of the sailors and pushed money in his hands, saying. 'Deliver this man safely to the beaches of Northumberland

and there will be more when you return.' She tucked a further £500 into Bateman's pocket and wished him well on his journey home. From the harbour wall she waved him farewell and reminded him of their promise. 'Seven years!' she cried.

When the seven years were up Sushy Pye dressed herself in her finest clothes and set sail for the north lands. On arriving in Northumberland, she disembarked and found herself walking through a rolling country full of sheep.

'Who owns this land?' she asked a lad with a crook in his hand. 'Lord Bateman,' came the reply. She looked at the far horizons and said. 'Where might I find his house?' The shepherd pointed to a mighty castle on a hill. 'A lady like you should not walk alone, I will take you there.'

A servant answered the castle door. 'I have come to see Lord Bateman,' she said. The man looked at her queerly. 'His lordship is busy preparing for his wedding tomorrow.' Sushy Pye turned to leave and then stopped; she took her half of the ring and placed it in the servant's hand.

'Give him this,' she said.

The servant ran up the winding stairway to Bateman, who was with his future wife and mother-in-law. Breathless, he said. 'There is a woman of the most extraordinary beauty, looking for you. Her jewellery alone could purchase half of Northumberland.'

The mother in law, looking at her daughter and then at Bateman, said. 'I am sure she cannot be more beautiful than your wife-to-be.'

But the servant would not be put off. 'She is undoubtedly the most beautiful woman I have ever seen. She gave me this to give to you.' He handed Bateman half the ring.

Seeing this, Bateman bounded, down the stairs, five at a time, so keen was he to behold Sushy Pye. When he reached the door, she turned away.

'I hear it is too late.'

'I will have no other than you,' said Bateman, taking her in his arms.

He climbed the stairs to his intended wife and mother in law and offered them a handsome package to return to London and say no more. The tears were many but useless.

Bateman started the day with one wife and ended it with another, for that day he married Sushy Pye.

Caedmon's Dream

Strictly speaking, one may ask what a story originating in Whitby, North Yorkshire, is doing in a book of Northumbrian Tales. Well, at the time of this tale in the seventh century, Whitby was part of Northumberland, a county which included everything north of the Humber up as far as Edinburgh.

Caedmon was a lay brother at Whitby Abbey at the time when St Hild was the abbess. He was a very pious man and spent his time praying and looking after the beasts in the abbey grounds.

In the evenings the brothers would quite often have ceilidhs, where there was much merry-making with drinking, singing and storytelling that went on late into the night. Caedmon would go to these out of duty but he was very often the first to leave because he was shy and had no stories or songs to offer.

One evening he was sitting amongst his merrymaking brothers when he saw the harp being passed toward him for a song. There was much laughter amongst his friends as they cried, 'play us a tune brother Caedmon'. Panic arose in his chest; he excused himself, got up and walked to the stable where he lay down with his beasts. He felt full of shame for his inadequacies, and it took him a long time to drift off to sleep. However, in his dreams a figure came and stood before him saying, 'Caedmon sing to me.' It was Caedmon's worst nightmare.

'I cannot,' said Caedmon. 'I do not know how to sing, it is why I left the ceilidh.'

'None the less, you shall sing for me,' the stranger said again.

'What do you want me to sing?' implored Caedmon.

'Sing of the beginning of things,' the man replied.

Caedmon opened his mouth and at once found he was singing verses in praise of God and his creation. The words flowed from his body like they had always been there. In the morning Caedmon remembered everything that had happened in his dream. He sang the song to himself and it flowed forth again.

He hurried to the reeve of Whitby and told him what had happened. The reeve immediately took the lay brother to Abbess Hild, who assembled a gathering of worthies and instructed Caedmon to recount his dream. They nodded and asked him to sing the song he was given.

> Now we must praise the Protector of the heavenly kingdom,
> The might of the Measurer and His mind's purpose,
> the work of the Father of Glory, as He for each of the wonders,
> the eternal Lord, established a beginning.
> He shaped first for the sons of men,
> heaven as a roof, the Holy Judge.
> Then the Middle-World, mankind's Guardian,
> the eternal Lord, made afterwards,
> solid ground for men, the almighty Lord.*

The abbess shook her head in wonder, indeed she said, 'Heavenly grace has been conferred upon you by the lord.'

All assembled spoke in agreement. She gave to him a piece of Holy Writ and asked that he put it into verse by the morning.

The following day Caedmon again sang and presented his songs in written verse. Abbess Hild immediately asked him to leave his secular life and be ordained as a monk. Caedmon spent the rest of his life putting the sacred history into verse.

He is believed to be the first recoded Anglo Saxon poet – all from the gift of a dream.

* Taken from Caedman's Hymn in Bede, with Judith McClure and Roger Collins (eds), *The Ecclesiastical History of the English People.*

THE SALMON AND THE RING

The salmon were almost eradicated from the Tyne through pollution during the Industrial Revolution. The river has now been cleaned up, and it is a great thrill to watch the salmon leaping up the weirs and waterfalls to return to their old spawning grounds. This particular story was in part inspiration for the tale of the 'Poacher' in the final chapter of the book.

The mayor of Newcastle, the alderman Francis Anderson, stood on the Tyne Bridge playing with his gold ring as he stared into the water. Presumably something was on his mind at the time for he absent-mindedly allowed the ring to fall from his finger and disappear into the dark, muddy depths of the great river below. It was a precious ring and the mayor felt a great despair realising there was very little chance of it ever being recovered.

One evening, later that week, his servant brought a salmon that he had caught in the river. On gutting the fish, he discovered the gold ring sparkling inside its stomach. He served the salmon on a plate to his master with the ring sitting on the side of the plate.

Over 100 years later, an ancestor of the alderman showed off the ring to a couple of antiquarians. It now had a salmon image engraved on the inside of the signet with the letters 'F' and 'A' (Francis Anderson) on either side of it.

7

WISE WOMEN, WITCHES AND WIZARDS

THE WITCH OF SEATON DELAVAL

This story clearly represents some fairly unsavoury politics. But it is a representation of a time. The very fact that the story was told is a tale in itself!

One evening at the end of April, Lord Delaval was riding home to Delaval Hall after a day in Newcastle. He was passing through Wallsend, when he noticed that there were men in the fields lighting fires and moving their cattle towards them.

'What are you doing?' he shouted to one man.

'It's May Eve,' the farmer called back. 'We are taking the cattle to the fires to cleanse them, there is much pestilence around.'

'Of course, May Eve, I had quite forgotten,' Delaval replied, more to himself than to anyone else. Each year the farmers would light big fires on May Day. They would sing and drive the beasts through the ashes to protect them from disease. The young Delaval did not approve of these ancient practices but the farmers were intent on carrying them out each year.

He continued his journey north and was just passing the dilapidated church of Holy Cross when he noticed the dancing flame of a candle reflected in a stained window. He was surprised and curious, so he dismounted and instead of opening the door, pulled himself up to look in the window. What he saw shook him. For inside was a circle of women, seated around a large black cauldron. They were incanting chants and spells, and one of them, whom he assumed was the leader, was dropping things into the pot, causing it to hiss and bubble.

Delaval let himself down on to the earth of the overgrown churchyard and, as quietly as he could, he crawled round and opened the church door. He edged himself forward across the floor and through the broken pews, to hear what they were saying.

'This is to cause sickness to the crops,' cackled one as she dropped a horrible looking object into the pot.

'This is so that the buds on the apple trees will wither and rot,' said another.

'May the cowherds' bones ache and ache and ache,' chuckled a third.

Now, whether Lord Delaval really heard these words or simply imagined what witches might say, we don't know, but he wanted to hear no more, so he leapt up and ran towards them. He tipped over the pot as the women scattered and disappeared into the night, but he managed to grab the chief of them and held her tightly. He bound her to the back of his horse and rode with her to Newcastle.

She was imprisoned for many days, and then on the testimony of Delaval, the woman was put on trial for witchcraft in Seaton Delaval. The prosecution read out a list of allegations against her.

The judge passed sentence. 'This woman is clearly a witch and should be burned at the stake for her evil activities,' he said over his glasses.

At this point there was a murmur in the crowd and neighbours of the woman started to protest. 'She should be shown leniency,' said one. 'She cured my child of the palsy.'

'Give her a last request,' said another.

The judge, seeing the mood of the crowd, nodded and said that she could have one last request.

The woman, who seemed quite unperturbed, turned and smiled. 'I would like two wooden plates,' she said.

There was a moment's silence and then a man rose and said: 'I'll bring what the woman wants. He was just leaving when she shouted after him, 'They must be unused!'

She was taken to the Seaton Delaval beach, where a stake had been erected and bundles of wood laid ready for the fire. The witch was made to stand by the stake, ready to have her hands tied before the fire was lit.

The man rushed over with two plates and handed them to the woman. She nodded her thanks and put one plate under each foot, intoning some words as she did so. Suddenly she rose into the air, flying off over the beach and out towards the sea.

'We are tricked!' said the judge.

'Wait and see,' said the man who brought the plates.

At that very moment, one plate dropped from the woman's foot. She keeled over and plunged into the salty water.

'I wondered if it might be trickery,' said the man. 'So I brought one plate that had been used a thousand times.'

As for the 'witch', she disappeared under the waves and was never seen again.

The Acklington Hare

Acklington is a small town not far from the Northumberland coast, which today is known for its men's prison, whilst in mediaeval times it was notorious for its witches. But who were these witches really?

The laird liked nothing better than to hunt with his horses, hounds and his entourage of followers. He would chase whatever animal came his way, be it the fox, the boar, the deer or the hare. Nancy Scott, on the other hand, liked to wander the woods, picking herbs, watching the animals and whispering in her low voice to whoever came her way – be they human or animal, natural or supernatural.

One Christmas time the laird had many guests staying in his castle. He had promised them good hunting but they had gone out day after day and caught nothing. He was angry and embarrassed.

So he decided one morning to go out alone and see what he could discover before he set out with his party on another futile chase. He rode his horse to a fork in the path and there he saw in front of him Nancy Scott sitting under a tree, on the other side of the track. He brought his horse to a stop.

'What are you doing here, Nancy Scott?' he said.

'Oh, this and that', she said. 'And a Merry Christmas to you, sir.'

'A Merry Christmas to you too, Nancy,' he said, caught a bit off his guard. 'There is not an animal to be seen is this place, do you know where they have gone?'

'I might or I might not,' she replied. 'For a silver sixpence, I could tell your lordship where to find a white hare.'

'I see no reason why I should pay you to find animals on my own land,' the laird retorted. Nancy shrugged her shoulders and said nothing.

The lord, in his frustration, put his hand into his britches and pulled out a coin, which he tossed to her. 'If there's nothing there, I'll see you hung,' he said.

Nancy merely pouted her lips and gave directions to a hollow on the moor above the woods. The laird rode straight back to his castle, whipping the backside of his horse as he went, his hound running at his side. He assembled his party and promised them that this day they would find good sport.

They all rode out in their fine Christmas clothes, horns blowing and hounds with their noses to the ground. The laird galloped off in front, leading the way to the hollow on the moor that Nancy Scott had spoken about. No sooner had they arrived there than a bright, white hare leapt from its cover and bounded off, darting in one direction and then the other. The dogs were soon on it, wild with the scent and hungry for a kill, the riders galloping not far behind. The hare sent the hunters on a merry chase, through the woods, up the hills and down the valleys. It was faster and trickier than any animal they had known and it seemed tireless.

One by one the hunters and hounds became exhausted and dropped back. Many gave up the chase altogether until eventually only the laird and his hound were still in the hunt. He had not paid a silver sixpence to be made to look a fool, and he spurred his horse on. The hare sped across the fields with the lord screaming behind it and the terrified hound on its tail. For a moment the hare stumbled and the hound lunged forwards grabbing its back leg. But the poor beast was too tired to hang on and the hare gave a mighty kick and was free, leaving the hound exhausted in the heather.

The hare shot off into the distance towards Acklington village. The laird spurred his horse on once more, now following the spots of blood left by the wounded animal on the grass and vegetation. The trail led him right the way to the back door of Nancy Scott's cottage.

The laird was astonished but he hammered on the door with his fist shouting, 'Nancy Scott, are you there?'

He barged open the door and marched in before she could reply. Nancy Scott was standing by the fire looking rather dishevelled, in her worn smock, sweat trickling down her brow.

'Give me that hare!' he bellowed.

'Is it right,' she said, 'for a gentleman to force his way into a lady's house, without a "by-your-leave"?' Nancy Scott admonished.

'The hare, where is it?' he said once more in a steely voice.

'There is no hare here my lord,' replied Nancy Scott. 'See for yourself.'

The lord searched Nancy Scott's house high and low, in cupboards and under beds, but for all his efforts he found nothing.

He scowled at her and walked to the door, but just before he left, he turned and noticed her sitting by the fire, her skirt raised as she dabbed ointment on a fresh wound on the back of her leg.

The laird shook his head and walked out mumbling and cursing.

Ji-Jaller Bag

This story takes place up the Tyne to the West of Newcastle, somewhere like Wylam or Ovingham where the old houses and allotments push down on to the river bank.

In a village near Newcastle, where the river Tyne rushed past people's doorsteps carrying the silver salmon from the sea and messages from all over the world, lived a strange old woman.

She had a large hooked nose, always wore black and shuffled around the streets in black slippers with sparkly things embroidered on the front. She looked exactly like your typical witch and some people said she was a witch but she could have just been a lonely old woman.

Whatever she was, she was definitely old and rheumatic. She had trouble bending down to pick up her dropped thimble and didn't have the energy to sweep the nooks and crannies like she used to.

So she put about the village that she needed a helper. Lots of young women thought about it, scratched their heads and wondered but only one knocked on the old woman's door. She was as haughty and as wily as the old woman herself. She would do as much work as was needed to get the few coins that the old woman would put into her palms but not a jot more!

Now, said the old woman, 'I want you to sweep the floor, cook the food, clean the pots and make the fire but never, ever put the broom up the chimney.'

Well, the girl had never thought about putting her broom up the chimney, what would she want to do that for? So she didn't – or not at first.

But when, on the fourth day, the old, crook-nosed woman said to the girl. 'Never, ever put your broom up the chimney.' The girl thought, 'Why not, what on earth could be up the chimney but a load of soot?'

So she waited until the old woman was busying herself with her buttons and bobbins and bits and pieces, and she shoved that broom right up the chimney. Down fell a long leather bag. She looked inside and it was full of sparking gold. Well, the girl didn't waste any time. She grabbed the ji-jaller bag (*whatever that is*) from the hook on the wall, put the long leather bag inside it, so as not to get it covered in soot and ran out the door and down the track.

The first thing she came to was a gate, and to her surprise the gate spoke in a creaky gate-like sort of way saying, 'Pretty maid will you open me, I've not been opened in many a year?' But the girl tossed her curly black locks in the air and said, 'Open yourself.'

She ran on until she came to a cow, which turned its head and looked at her in a doleful cow-like sort of way and said, 'Pretty maid, will you milk me, I've not been milked in many a year?' But she tossed her curly black locks in the air and said, 'Milk yourself.'

Eventually she came to an old, tattered mill, which said in a tired out sort of way, 'Pretty maid, will you turn me, I've not been turned in many a year?' Again, the girl tossed her curly black locks in the air and said. 'Turn yourself.'

When she entered the mill, she was exhausted with all the running and refusing she had been doing, so she curled up beside her bag in the mill hopper and fell asleep.

When the old woman realised what her maid had done, she hurried out of the house with her stick in her hand and followed that crooked nose of hers right down the track.

She came to the gate and said, 'Gate o' mine, gate o' mine, have you seen a maid o' mine with a ji-jaller bag, a long leather bag and all the money I ever had?' To which the gate replied, 'Straight ahead.'

She came to the cow and said, 'Cow o' mine, cow o' mine. Have you seen a maid o' mine with a ji-jaller bag, a long leather bag and all the money I ever had?' to which the gate replied, 'Straight ahead.'

When she reached the mill she said, 'Mill o' mine, mill o' mine. Have you seen a maid o' mine with a ji-jaller bag, a long leather bag and all the money I ever had?' to which the gate replied, 'In the hopper.'

Now the old woman saw the girl curled up amongst the grain, took her bag and hobbled off back down the track, smiling to herself.

Of course it was not long before the hook-nosed crone lost her bobbin under the bed and realised she needed another maid.

Well, this time the girl that came was quiet and thoughtful and took the job to earn a few pence so she could buy her old father a new pair of boots.

'I want you to sweep the floor, cook the food, clean the pots, and make the fire but never, ever put the broom up the chimney,' said the old crone. Now the quiet one thought quietly to herself that she had never considered putting her broom up the chimney until that moment and forgot all about it.

But when on the fourth day the old one said to her, 'Never, ever put your broom up the chimney.' She became very curious, because she was that sort of girl. She waited until all was clear and she quietly poked that broom right up the chimney and you know what fell down: a bag of gold of course!

She grabbed the ji-jaller bag from the wall and went off down the track. Well, the first thing she came to was that very same gate which said, 'Pretty maid, will you open me, for I have not been opened in many a year?'

The girl, who was quite different from the first one, said. 'Of course I will.' She opened the gate and the gate sighed a soft 'Thank you.'

Well the same thing happened with the cow and the mill. She milked the one and turned the other, and each whispered 'Thank you,' in its own way. The girl was so tired with all that opening, milking and turning that she lay down in the mill hopper, curled up with the bag and fell asleep.

When the old woman realised what had happened for the second time, she was out down the track with her stick, following her crooked nose.

She came to the gate and said. 'Gate o' mine, gate o' mine. Have you seen a maid o' mine with a ji-jaller bag, a long leather bag and all the money I ever had?' But this time the gate said nothing.

The same thing happened with the cow and the mill, so the old woman had no idea where to go. She followed that crooked nose of hers in a crooked sort of way round and round in circles and as far as I know she still is.

Whatever happened, she never found that quiet girl who was curled up in the mill hopper. That girl eventually woke up and found herself with a ji-jaller bag full of gold, which I have no doubt she was very happy about. What she did with it is anybody's guess, but I do know her dad needed a new pair of shoes.

MEG OF MELDON

Just west of Morpeth along the Hartburn is Meldon Hall, now the home of a tasteful cafe and garden centre. It was, however, once the abode of one of the most infamous of Northumbrian women. Many a story has been told by a winter's fire about Meg of Meldon, but who was she, this woman that was variously called a business woman, a witch, a miser and a ghost? This story gives an account of Meg's mysterious activities, leading to the folk legend of Meg and the Well.

There certainly was an historical Meg: Margaret Selby, born in 1570, who inherited a lot of interest on land from her wealthy father. Meg was beautiful, rich and a prize for any man, and it wasn't surprising that William Fenwick of Wallington Hall was keen to marry her. They made their match, and whilst it was undoubtedly sweet for a while, Meg was said to be mean and ruthless. Her gentle husband could not cope with her and departed to an early grave.

Meg then set her teeth into others. She disinherited Heron, the young man who owned Meldon Hall, by demanding the return of a large loan at short notice and forcing him to give her the property as collateral. Meldon Hall under her belt, she decided to get her hands on Hartington Hall a few miles up the Hartburn. Again she demanded the immediate return of a substantial loan that the owners could not repay and made that hall part of her portfolio too.

Perhaps she was just a very good business woman and the men could not cope with a woman beating them at their own game, but it is at this point that the historical Meg turns into something else. It was said that she travelled between her two premises, Hartington Hall and Meldon Hall, by a subterranean coach, which she entered through the Battling Stone in the middle of the Hartburn River, a place where women used to 'beat the lie out of their webs' in the bleaching season. All the farmers' land along the course of the river became sickly whilst Meg's land thrived. People were not happy with this! She was not going to have an ordinary death.

When Meg died, she left no money, despite her enormous wealth and was condemned to live, alternately, seven years of peace and seven years of restless wandering. During this time she was seen in many guises.

'There goes Meg', people would say when they saw the flicker of coloured lights beneath the beech trees above the river. She would be seen as a beautiful young woman dressed in white. But there was also a little black dog that ran along the parapet of Meldon Bridge. She was often seen further down the river at Newminster Abbey, where she would sit dolefully on the side of a stone coffin, head in hands.

What was she doing in these places? Was she watching over the vast treasures she had left behind? One day in Meldon School, the master left his pupils to go for lunch, and whilst they were taking their 'bait' from their satchels, the ceiling fell in and with it came a leather bag full of coins, which scattered over the floor. The boys filled their pockets with Meg's fortune and never a word was said, until much later.

Another group of children were playing in the Meldon Tower, known then as the 'ruinous castle', when one of them dislodged a stone. Underneath they found a hoard of gold with which they filled their hats and caps. But they say it was evil money, so no good ever came from it.

MEG AND THE WELL

Perhaps there was another side to Meg. For one night a poor countryman had a dream. He dreamed of a bullskin bag of gold at the bottom of a well. He was told to go there at the stroke of midnight and that there would be a person there to help him. He would retrieve the gold, so long as he said not a word and made no sound.

The farmer awoke both excited and terrified. If the dream were true, he could become a gentleman for the rest of his life. But he also knew that it was dangerous to play with hidden treasure. He told nobody and did nothing for a few days, then one day he passed by the well and flicked in a stone. He waited and there was no splash, only a dull thud when it hit the bottom. At least he wouldn't drown.

That night he resolved to give it a go. It was winter, so he dressed well, then gathered a coil of rope and tied some hooks to the bottom. He walked quietly to the well with only starlight as his companion. He noticed the shadow of a figure that seemed to be waiting for him and hesitated. But the figure came towards him, his face hidden by a hood. The stranger guided him to the well-side. The farmer opened his mouth to thank him and quickly shut it, remembering the condition of silence.

Together they tied the rope to the jack reel above the well and, careful to make no noise, they began to lower it. A few turns down the stranger tied a loop in the rope, into which the farmer put his leg. He was then lowered into the pitch darkness. At the bottom he felt around and there indeed was the bulging bullskin bag. Careful not to rustle his jacket or jingle the coins, he attached the hooks. The stranger began to winch the farmer back up, the bag dangling below him.

When he reached the lip of the well he jumped nimbly on to the wall whilst the stranger continued turning the jack handle.

The bag appeared, the countryman reached out to grab it. As his hands touched the hide he muttered, 'And now we have her!' The words acted like a dissolving spell and the bag slipped from his hands and hurtled back into the darkness without a sound. The figure beside him sighed, and the farmer looked around to see not a man but Meg of Meldon, her eyes both wild and sorrowful as she too faded away.

The farmer never did become a gentleman and never returned to the well. But perhaps that is just as well for they do say that no good ever came from evil-got money.

THE RELUCTANT TIDE

Morpeth, whose name means 'murder path or path of the dead', is one of the biggest market towns in Northumberland. It is situated some eight miles from the sea along the River Wansbeck. The Mitchell Scott of this story is the famous wizard Michael Scott of Scotland, who appears to have been a real figure of great learning and influence in his time.

The good burgers of Morpeth had long been jealous of Newcastle for its tidal river on which boats could enter the heart of the town. For goods to reach Morpeth, however, they had to be unloaded at Cambois and tediously transported by wagon overland.

The burgers dreamed of the waters of the Wansbeck lapping outside the Morpeth Chantry, with its little quay, from which cargo from across the world could be unloaded. One wet and windy afternoon a conversation began amongst a group of them in the town hall.

'Think of the riches we would earn, if we could persuade the tide to flow into Morpeth,' one said.

Another laughed. 'That would be like splitting a mountain in two, no man can do that.'

'There is one who can,' said a third. 'The mighty wizard Mitchell Scott; was he not responsible for splitting the Eildon Hills?'

Everyone knew of Mitchell Scott, as the most powerful wizard in all the land.

'He is the Devil's piper! They say it was he and the devil that built the mighty wall from Newcastle to Carlisle in less than a day,' said the mayor.

The others nodded.

'And was it not Mitchell Scott that rode his black stallion to France to demand that the king stop the French pirates attacking our ships? The French nobility laughed at him at first but Scott then commanded his great horse to stamp its hooves and every steeple in Paris trembled, clanging its bells out loud,' said the clerk.

'Aye and the pirate raids stopped after that,' added another.

'If anyone can make the tide come to Morpeth, he is the one. We will seduce him with our fine buildings, food and hospitality,' said the mayor firmly.

The group dispersed, each person thinking of their own vessel sitting in the Morpeth quay, with its rigging catching the breeze and their pockets full of foreign coins.

One day a mighty thundering was heard that caused the rocks to stir and tumble on the far distant Rothley Crags. There was a cloud of dust and riding into Morpeth on his black stallion was none other than Mitchell Scott.

A reception committee was quickly gathered and the burgers wined and dined the great man in the finest hostelries of Morpeth. When all were relaxed and merry, Mitchell Scott turned to the mayor and said, 'And what is it you want of me, good fellow?'

The mayor took a deep breath and said: 'Sir, it would help us greatly if the tide flowed to Morpeth, might you be able to help us in this matter?'

Mitchell Scott raised his eyebrows. 'An unusual request,' he smiled. 'Difficult but not impossible, how far are we from the sea?'

'Under a dozen miles as the River Wansbeck flows,' the clerk replied quickly.

'It will need a young person of speed and courage to achieve this. Can you bring me such a one?'

There was some jostling amongst the burgers as to whose son, grand-daughter nephew or niece would get the honour but

eventually one was chosen, and a bright, fast-running young man was brought to meet Mitchell Scott. The great wizard spoke to him in front of the assembled company.

'Go to the place where the river meets the sea. There you must wait until the tide rises to its fullest. You must then turn and run without stopping and without fear until you reach Morpeth town,' said the great wizard, 'and on no account must you look behind.'

The young man took a deep breath and jogged to the river mouth, where he waited as the sun gently rose over the sea. A fisherman nodded his head. 'The tide will rise no further,' he said.

The young man began to run the dozen miles into Morpeth following the twists and turns of the river. At first he noticed nothing except the pounding of his feet on the wet grass, and then as he was running through Sleekburn, he felt the water lapping at his heels.

He ran faster, but now he could hear it splashing and feel small waves reaching up to his calves. Still he put on speed but it only seemed to make the sea wilder. He entered the village of Sheepwash and heard a great roar behind him like a mighty wave. It broke, soaking his back. He heard the water gather strength again and began to hear the cries and yells of the water sprites who did not want to come inland: this was not their world. He sprinted to the bend in the river at Bothal, and now his heart was beating hard. He was only four miles short of Morpeth when a wave rose behind him and as it crashed past his ear, there was a wild scream. In fear of what was coming next, the lad turned his head and glanced behind, but immediately he did so the gathering wave lost its momentum and the water retreated backward as if it was being sucked into the sea. The young man turned and sped on but it was too late and no water followed him. The spell was broken and the tide withdrew back to the great ocean, never to rise so far again.

Mitchell Scott left Morpeth as he found it – a town without a harbour – and so it is to this day. The tide comes up the Wansbeck River only as far as Bothal.

8

GHOSTS AND
UNQUIET SOULS

THE GHOSTLY BRIDAL PARTY OF FEATHERSTONEHAUGH

This story happens at Featherstone in the South Tyne valley. Featherstone is thought to mean the place of a dolmen, a stone-age structure comprising three standing stones with a capstone. Now there is a castle and the remains of a prisoner of war camp. It has long been a place of power. At a recent marriage ceremony in the castle grounds, a version of this story was told, but fortunately the bride and groom managed to escape in a waiting canoe – their wedding present. The tale lives on.

Abigail, the only daughter of Baron de Featherstonehaugh, was wild and free-spirited. One day she met a young man whose heart beat to the same fierce tune as hers. The two of them galloped across the moors like a couple of falcons playing in the wind. They met often and love between them grew. It was easy for them to meet, for he was of the Ridley household, a short ride across the common to Featherstone.

When Abigail's father saw what was happening, he seethed with anger. How dare this wastrel interfere with his plans? Ridley had neither the property nor the standing to be a suitable match for his daughter. The baron already had a beau in mind for her and he wasn't a Ridley; he was a Featherstonehaugh.

The baron tried to persuade his daughter of the wisdom of his choice with words like 'prospects', 'property' and 'position', and for a lady of that time these things mattered. But Abigail was as stubborn and as forceful as her father.

'He is DULL,' she cried 'and I do not love him!'

'You can learn to,' her father replied, 'I will not have you marrying that worthless varmint Ridley, and squandering my estate.'

'I care nothing for your estate,' she said. 'What if I refuse?'

'You will marry my choice and that's an end to it. I ban you from seeing that Ridley fellow again.'

He strode off and set about arranging the marriage between his daughter Abigail and Timothy Featherstonehaugh.

Abigail, however, flouted her father's wishes and continued to gallop through the woods and hills with Ridley up to the day of her marriage.

The reluctant bride was led up the isle in Haltwhistle church in the arm of her victorious father. A great celebration was prepared at Featherstone Castle, with the best musicians and mountains of exquisite food.

As was the custom, the baron suggested that the bride and groom, together with the bridal party, beat the bounds of their new estate to mark their territory and show off their wealth. On their return, the great feast would be ready.

The ladies and gentlemen, dressed in their finery, rode from Featherstone to Eals; from Eals across the fells to Coanwood and from Coanwood through the woods to Ramshaw. Here they crossed the Tyne into the wooded valley of Pinkyn's Cleugh. As they entered the wood, all was uncannily quiet, conversation stopped and the guests looked around warily. Then, from out of the trees, the Ridley boys appeared, armed with knives and swords and Abigail's lover at the front.

'Hand her over,' he shouted. 'It's me she wants and me she shall have!'

It was all supposed to be so easy. Frighten off the unwary party and abscond with Abigail to the hills and over the border. But that is not what happened. The bridal party, sensing trouble, already

had their hands to their swords and instead of retreating, attacked their ambushers. There was a bloody battle.

Man slaughtered man until, in the height of the frenzy, Timothy Featherstone lunged his sword toward Ridley. Abigail, seeing what was happening, leapt in between the two men, but Featherstone did not see in time and the thrust entered her breast and into the heart of her lover as well. She was killed at the hand of her groom. Timothy Featherstone, in shame and despair, fell on his sword. Not one person left Pinkin's Cleugh alive that afternoon and only the watching mighty oaks knew the truth of what happened. They still stand there, holding their silence.

At the castle, Baron de Featherstonehaugh had the bells rung for the start of the feast but the bridal party never came. He sent out riders to give them notice but none were found. He waited and waited, anxiety mounting in his huge frame. Guests left, musicians fell asleep, and the finely cooked goose and the crane became cold and congealed. Then at the stroke of midnight, he heard the sound of hooves. The baron sat up. In through the great castle doors rode the bridal party, still on their horses. They dismounted one by one and took their places around the table, each one translucent white, with terrible wounds around their face and neck. As the Baron stared in horror, he saw the face of his daughter, and the others seated around her, slowly fade away until the hall was left quite silent and empty. The only sound was that of the sobbing lord, crouched over the festive table, his head in his hands.

Outside in Pinkyn's Cleugh a raven drank from a hollow in the raven's stone, where the blood of the lover had dripped.

That was on 17 January. It is said that each evening on this date, the ghostly bridal party can be seen entering the castle and taking their seats at the banqueting table.

THE WHITE LADY OF BLENKINSOPP

The crumbling walls of Blenkinsopp Castle now stand in the middle of a village of sixty-one holiday homes, just south of Hadrian's Wall.

Bryan de Blenkinsopp was a great fighter, a handsome and fearless man, admired by many. Musicians sang to him and ladies courted him. But he had a dark, secret desire that haunted him. Although one of the wealthiest men in Northumberland, he was compulsive in his desire to accumulate ever more wealth.

One day, he was attending the wedding of a friend when a toast was made to Bryan that he should soon marry his lady love. Perhaps it was the ale that loosened his tongue to reveal the poisoned soul inside, but he could contain his secret no longer. He thumped his fist on the table and declared, 'I will marry no woman unless she brings with her a chest of gold that will take ten of my strongest man to carry!'

Everyone at the table looked around with a mixture of shock and disgust at their friend. Bryan read the feelings in their eyes and immediately regretted his words, but they could not be unsaid. It was, after all, his truth. The next day, he was overtaken by shame; he could not face seeing anyone and left at dawn to go far away. He decided to fight in the Crusades for king and country, where there was the possibility of acquiring largesse beyond his dreams.

It was some years later that he returned to Blenkinsopp Castle and he came with his prize. A dark skinned woman from a far-away exotic world. And with her she brought a chest that took twelve of his strongest men to carry.

His friends and neighbours nodded their heads. 'He has what he wanted, and may it bring him happiness!' But happiness it did not bring. Bryan's wife, wanting to be sure that he had not married her solely for her wealth, hid her treasure in the vaults beneath the castle. She would not allow him to touch it without her consent. If there was one thing worse than not having wealth, it was having wealth that he could not get his hands on. Bryan de Blenkinsopp felt demeaned.

Stories soon spread of constant arguing in the couple's home. The people looked at his new wife askance; she was strange, not one of them. Her entourage spoke a foreign tongue and she, herself, was difficult to understand, dressing in clothes from another world. People were suspicious of her. Words began to be passed around the villages on the banks of the River Tipault, which were as ignorant as they were malicious. People began to think that she had come to ensnare Bryan's soul.

Whether she ensnared Bryan de Blenkinsopp's soul or not, he could bear his impotence no longer and suddenly disappeared, leaving not a trace behind him. His wife searched but could not find him. She became isolated and remorseful, regretting the way she had treated her husband. She sent her people out far and wide to bring him home. But it was all to no avail, he was nowhere to be found.

For some time, the woman rattled around in the house with her huge wealth, but one day she left too. Neither returned to Blenkinsopp Castle; its walls remained empty, holding only the secrets of whatever had passed between them. Slowly the old place began to crumble with loss and neglect.

Many years later, the gardener, who lived in some apartments in the crumbling building, heard his child screaming from his bedroom in the middle of the night. He ran to the boy's bedside and found his son sitting bolt upright in his bed, perspiration running down his face.

'The white lady, the white lady!' the boy cried.

'There's no white lady here, you must have been dreaming,' his father replied.

'No,' said the boy. 'She was here, right here. She came and sat on the side of the bed and said she needed my help.' The boy choked then found his breath. 'I was very frightened but she looked sad, so I felt sorry for her. She said that long ago, she hid some precious treasure in the vaults of the castle that has caused her much suffering and she could not rest, until she had recovered it.'

'What did she want from you,' his father said softly, seeing that the child now spoke more calmly the truth of what had happened.

'She said she needed a living soul to accompany her to the vaults and that she would like me to be the one. I wanted to but I was scared and shook my head. Then she kissed me softly and said she would carry me and leant forwards to pick me up. That is when I panicked and screamed. I heard your footsteps, and when I looked up, she had disappeared.'

For several more nights the white lady came to the child but eventually his mother and father moved him to another room and she came no more. The child, on becoming an adult, always remembered the cold touch of the white lady's lips on his cheek.

Later on, barmen of the pub saw a woman walking through the walls but never again did she speak.

Evidence of the white lady appeared once more when a farmer was clearing some rubble round the castle. He came across a musty tunnel entrance that was buzzing with flies. The old stories were reignited and the word of the white lady's treasure spread though the community. Many gathered to stare into the underground portal. At first no one would enter, then one man, an ex-miner, stepped up and said he did not fear. He was handed a candle and lowered himself into the pitch dark of the dank mouldering entrance. He followed a passage down a flight of steps to a door that once barred the way. Its planks were now rotten, hanging uselessly from their hinges. The passage turned sharply and he came to another flight of steps, spiralling downwards. He held out the candle to see better but a draft of foul smelling air blew up from the depths and the flame was extinguished. The man emerged from the tunnel sometime later, his body trembling and his face ashen white. Another ventured inside with a canary, but no sooner had he reached the spiral staircase than the bird collapsed in its cage. He too emerged shaking his head. No one ever went back down there again and the new landowners sealed it up.

The stories haven't stopped, however. An exotic-looking woman arrived sometime ago, saying that she had had a dream in which she had seen the castle with its hoard of treasure. She asked for information from the local inn-keeper, requesting that he tell no one of her visit. She stayed for some time, but the owner of the castle was unwilling to let her investigate. Gossip once more spread through the community, and she too disappeared and was not seen again.

There are links with another castle, Thirwall Castle a mile and a half across the river.

THIRWALL CASTLE

Baron John Thirwall returned from the Crusades with treasure. A gold table, inlaid with jewels. It was his biggest pride and source of fame and notoriety. Far from being hidden, this treasure was ostentatiously displayed. People were invited to dine and play cards on the table. It was the most coveted and sought after piece of furniture in the borders, and Sir John looked after it well. Some say it was guarded by a dwarf servant of strange, unaccountable origins.

One day a determined band of Scots attacked the baron's castle, breaking down the mighty oak doors and rampaging into the room where the table was kept. When they arrived, however, they saw nothing save for a small dark figure disappearing with something shining above his head.

'I will keep the table safe for you and none other than you!' it shouted as it ran.

It then leapt into the castle well and sealed it after, leaving no trace of the entrance behind it. Sir John died in the battle, and the ancient well was nowhere to be seen. Many have tried to find this hidden portal and many have called out the name of the dwarf but he remains stubbornly hidden. It seems that it will remain that way forever so long as the little man is loyal to his promise to Sir John to return it to none other than he.

Whilst excavating around Thirwall Castle they found an underground tunnel, which was almost certainly a secret passage between Thirwall and Blenkinsopp. Could there be a link between the two stories? The stories are very similar, so it makes sense. Both tales are about treasures brought back from foreign wars, guarded over by exotic strangers and hidden underground; both still exerting their influence on the places … neither found nor likely to be.

THE UNFORTUNATE MINSTREL OF BELLISTER

This story came to being in the time of the border reivers, a few hundred years later than the white lady of Blenkinsopp Castle. A time when there was continuous strife in the border lands both between England and Scotland and one family and the next. It was a time of suspicion and mistrust, when a wary eye had to be kept on everyone, friend or foe.

One winter's evening, a long time ago, a grey haired minstrel wandered along the banks of the Tyne, wondering where he might find sustenance for his belly and a place to lay his head. The chill was beginning to bite into his bones when he noticed, between the trees, the lights of an imposing castle. He quickened his step and walked towards it, already imagining warming his feet by the hearth of a roaring fire and a jug of beer in his hand. It was tradition to offer hospitality to minstrels in return for a song or a story. He was not to know, however, that this was Bellister Castle, occupied at the time by the ill-fated Blenkinsopp family.

The minstrel pulled the iron handle of the bell and heard a voice from inside asking his business. He played some notes on his pipes and sang his request for hospitality. The door was opened and he was welcomed inside to a place at the table in the great hall, where the company were feasting. Like a dream, he found himself seated in front of a plate of hot food and a jug of beer. Slowly the warmth returned to his fingers and his belly glowed with ample portions of greasy food and considerable quantities of ale. Eventually the minstrel got up and sat beside the blazing fire. He fitted his pipes, loosed his tongue, stamped his foot and obliged the company with tales, ballads and praise songs, each one skilfully chosen to flatter his hosts and gently follow the ebb and flow of the evening. [014]

The ale flowed, and the revelry unfolded to everyone's satisfaction. The baron, however, who had begun the evening very much enjoying the entertainment, started to see things that he had not before noticed. It may well have been a result of his beery haze but it seemed to him that the minstrel's face changed from old to young and from innocent to devious. Suddenly a seed of doubt entered him. 'What if this man was a spy sent from across the border? Perhaps he was a crafty thief who had inveigled himself into his house.' The minstrel noticed the baron's shift of countenance and himself began to feel uncomfortable, moving uneasily in his seat, his fingers missing notes. This added to the baron's suspicions, his eyes narrowed and he began to think that perhaps this minstrel was an assassin, come to cut their throats as they slept.

The musician, who could now hardly take his eyes off the agitated gaze of the baron, felt a surge of panic run through his body and suddenly announced that he was tired after his long journey and wished to be shown to his sleeping quarters. One of the servants obliged and led him down the long corridors to his bed chamber. The ceilidh wound down and slowly the household dispersed to their own beds.

But the baron could not sleep, certain that this man meant him harm. He asked a servant to take him to the minstrel's room, but when he entered, he found it empty and the man gone. Now, more convinced than ever that the minstrel was up to no good, he took his hounds out into the cold night air and told them to seek the stranger out. It was not long before they found the poor fellow crouched and shivering by the banks of the Tyne. The dogs, in their excitement, attacked the man, tearing into his flesh. By the time the baron arrived, he was lying limply on the ground. The baron left him there, certain that now he could do no harm.

The following morning, when the alcohol had cleared from the lord's head, he realised what had happened in the night and rushed out to find the minstrel. But when he saw him, he was stone cold dead. Being essentially a good man, the baron was ashamed of what he had done and had the minstrel buried just outside the castle walls.

One night as he was walking home, he passed the grave and saw the grey man sitting, desolately playing his pipes. The baron's heart leapt and he approached the figure, but as he did so it faded away. He saw him often after that and each time the apparition disappeared. The Baron entered into a great torment, not being able to forgive himself for the murder of an innocent old man, and he too went to an early grave.

That was not the last of the minstrel, however, for many years later a young man was walking up from the Tyne to take employment in the castle. It was rapidly becoming dark when he noticed a figure up ahead of him. He was keen to catch up and accompany the person, for they were clearly going in the same direction, but no matter how fast the young man walked, the figure was always ahead. Eventually he started to run but still the figure glided in front of him. This was all the more disconcerting when he noticed it had long grey hair and a grey cape. They eventually reached the door of the castle where the grey haired one turned around and the youth saw the terrible figure of an old man with horrible gashes and wounds about his body.

The apparition slowly faded away and the terrified youth knocked on the door of his new employ. He told the servant about his experience and she nodded her head sadly telling the young man the tragic tale of The Unfortunate Minstrel of Bellister. She went on to say that this vision was seldom seen without it being followed by a tragedy, and indeed that is exactly what happened, for that night the youth succumbed to a terrible fever and never woke up.

OLAF THE VIKING PRIOR

This story is from Tynemouth Priory and Castle, a dramatic building perched on cliffs at the mouth of the Tyne.

Olaf was part of a Viking raid on Tynemouth. He fought hard but was badly wounded in the battle. His brothers, fleeing for their own lives, left him for dead and sailed on to see what booty they might find in less well guarded monasteries along the Tyne.

Olaf, however, was not dead, though he was sure he soon would be and hauled himself into the hollow of a sand dune, out of sight of the Saxon British. It was better to die in solitude than at the sword of his enemy. Olaf was out of luck, however, for a monk from the priory who was on the lookout for more invaders, almost stumbled over his slouched body. The monk looked down at the Norseman whose blood, he could see, was seeping into the sands and pushed him with his toe to check if he was still alive. He had a mind to finish him off, if he was. Olaf opened his eyes and looked up at the man, waiting for the blows.

But the monk stayed his hand, for what he saw looking up at him was the face of fear. He took pity on his enemy. Instead, he reached down and helped him stand and became his crutch as he led him back to the priory.

Olaf had always lived by the law of Odin and the raven. He had no belief in Christianity or the Church, which he simply saw as institutions of great wealth, ripe for the taking. In the priory, however, the monks dressed his wounds and prayed for his soul whilst he slowly recovered. Olaf decided to convert to this seemingly benign religion and stayed in the priory at Tynemouth, progressing to the position of prior. People forgot his origins as he became one of them.

One day shouts rang around the priory once more: 'The Norsemen are come back!' People from the villages all around poured into the priory for protection, armed with scythes, pitchforks – whatever came to hand. The doors were bolted, and Olaf ordered the wary brothers to position themselves for the attack.

It was Eric the Viking who pounded on the door. 'Open up,' he shouted, 'Or we'll tear the place down.' The brothers held their ground. Then the Vikings made a full scale assault, pounding at the door until it burst open. The monks were ready with boulders and hot oil, which they threw down over their invaders' heads.

As luck would have it, one boulder fell full on Eric's back, crushing him into the ground. His men, seeing that their leader was fatally wounded, panicked and ran back to their boats. Olaf went down to attend to the wounded man, just as he had been helped in times gone by, but when he held the man's head in his hands, he recognised the face of his own brother. Tears poured down his face, to the bemusement of his waiting monks, and Eric died in his arms.

Olaf entered into a great state of melancholy after that and followed his brother to the grave. Today you might see the ghost of Olaf standing out on the cliffs beneath the ruined priory, staring out to sea.

NELLY THE KNOCKER

This is a story from near Haltwhistle that may have echoes of our ancient past. There is evidence that the early Stone-Age farmers may have believed that certain stones had spirits and were able to walk. These stones often covered great treasure or were portals into other worlds.

Outside of Haltwhistle there was a large standing stone that had been there for a very long time. At night a soft knocking could be heard coming from this boulder. Everyone knew what it was. It was Nelly the Knocker, sitting on the top, tap-tap-tapping with a pebble. Those that saw her reported that she always wore the same clothes and had the same demeanour. She was hunched over the boulder as if waiting for it to talk, wearing her black dress and black headscarf, like the women of the olden days.

Nobody minded her, least of all the farmer for whom she was a comfort and a companion. People wondered if anything lay beneath the stone. But they did not want to disturb Nelly, so left it alone.

Then the farmer died, and the farm was sold to another man with two sons. He was told about Nelly but didn't really believe, thinking it was superstition of the backward people of those parts. But no sooner had he settled in than he heard the same knocking and there, sitting atop the boulder, was Nelly. He was surprised and shook his head in bemusement but let it pass.

His two sons were more curious and they crept out night after night to watch Nelly at her business. They wanted to know what, if anything, was under that stone. So one day they asked a quarryman who had expertise with gunpowder to show them how to lay a charge and light a fuse. They waited until the daytime, when Nelly could not be seen, and they put down the explosive and blew up the mighty rock, shattering it into fragments and leaving a great hole in the ground.

When they cleared away the debris from the hole, they found three clay pots full of silver coins. They were rich and Nelly was never seen again. Whether the fortune made them happy, we do not know.

THE SILKIE OF BLACK HEDDON

This story takes place in the gently undulating low-lying land north of Hadrian's Wall.

The Silkie of Black Heddon got her name from the black silks she wore that rustled in the night. She stayed close to water and could often be heard by the meanders of the Black Heddon Burn, flitting amongst the silhouettes of the trees and tip-toeing across the ripples. She liked to sit on the bridge staring intently into the depths, dreaming up mischief. It was said that she was mean and malevolent, intent on causing whatever misery she could.

The Black Heddon Silkie had a particular penchant for horses. She would wait for people to ride across the bridge and then jump on to a horse's back, behind its rider. This would cause the horse to panic and gallop wildly in any direction, so the rider would have to hold on for dear life. Very often the only thing that would make the horse stop was when it died of exhaustion.

On other occasions, she would invisibly bar a horse's way so that it would come to a sudden stop and refuse to go on. One particular rider was off to the market to meet an important client when his mount stopped. The man could not understand it and spent a very long time trying to persuade the horse to move. He tried talking sweetly to it, hitting it with his crop and digging in his heels but all to no avail. The light began to fail and he became very anxious, perspiration flowing down his brow.

He may well have stayed there until the first light of the morning if a knowing local hadn't seen what was going on and come to his rescue. The local brought a piece of rowan wood, which he rubbed down the animal's flanks, freeing it from the Silkie's spell. The horse immediately continued its journey as if nothing had happened.

The Silkie loved to haunt the crags by Belsay Hall, where her favourite spot was a little pond from which flowed a stream. This stream tumbled over a waterfall and there beneath it stood a contorted tree, its twisted boughs hanging over the burn.

The Silkie had a seat that hung from one of these boughs and she would often be seen by night swinging to and fro over the water.

The Silkie was associated with death but nobody knew if she foretold death or caused it. One elderly woman calmly told the priest that she would soon die as the Silkie had come and sat on the end of her bed. Three days later she passed away.

Like Meg of Meldon, people said that this spectre had a great hidden fortune and that is why she couldn't rest. This may well have been true, for one day the ceiling of an old farmhouse in Black Heddon collapsed and amongst the fallen rubble was a black dog's skin full of gold. After that the Silkie was never seen again.

Who was this woman? Was she the manifestation of people's fears of the night? Was she an unquiet soul who haunted people's imaginations? Perhaps she was both of these but it may also be possible that she was a descendent of the pagan gods of the ancient Celts who inhabited these waterways in times past.

9

THE UNSEEN
AND THE SLY

CALALLY CASTLE

Calally is a secret place. The road from Rothbury goes though Lorbottle,
where the men tried to capture a cuckoo to make summer last forever,
and on to Dancing Hall, where the fairy folk once lived. Calally village
is surrounded by woodland under the rocky outcrop of Calally Crags.
In the valley below are the remnants of an old a motte and bailey
castle, whilst above it, on Castle Hill, are the impressive remains of
an Iron Age fort hiding amongst the contorted forms of ancient beech
trees. On excavating the hill fort, archaeologists found signs of a later
structure that had been built on top of it – Calally Castle? High on the
crags there is a beautiful cave carved out of a rock by a religious man
for meditation and prayer. It is a place full of mysteries. Such is the case
with this story.

There was once a lord and lady of Calally who wanted to build a
new residence for themselves, whether it was to be a castle, a palace
or perhaps just a fine mansion. Whatever it was, they couldn't
agree whether it was to go on top of the hill or down in the valley.

The lady wanted the castle built in the peaceful valley where
she could enjoy the song of the birds and walk out on a summer's
day sheltered from the winds. Her husband, the lord, on the other
hand, wanted it built on top of the hill where he would be able to

look out at the fine views over to the Cheviots and cast his eyes over his extensive lands.

The two of them dillied and dallied for a long time, each soliciting allies to their point of view, but they still could not agree. Eventually, however, the lord decided he would have his way, regardless of her. He employed the best mason in the area and instructed him to draw up plans for the finest of buildings. Materials were ordered and carried up to the top of Castle Hill.

There, on the ramparts of what had once been an Iron Age fort, they dug the foundations and started to build the walls of a great castle. The lord watched and he was happy with what he saw. It was definitely the right thing to do, to build the castle on the hill!

The following morning, however, the stones of the carefully laid walls were scattered to all corners of the mound. The lord was furious and blamed the master mason for poor workmanship.

'It needs to be strong and mighty to withstand the worst of gales,' he shouted.

So the men started again. The mason was very careful about how they placed the stones, and he watched them like a hawk. At the end of the day they had built the walls higher and more substantial than the day before. The workmen trooped down the hill, retired to a hearty meal and went to their beds satisfied. Come the morning, however, the stones of the walls were scattered again.

The men began to mutter about supernatural forces, but the lord was determined not to be beaten. He cracked the whip and insisted that they build again. He even employed a new master mason to supervise the job.

Again they laboured hard and the walls were built even higher and stronger than on the second day. But, again, by morning time the walls were down.

The following day the lord insisted they build once more, but that night he sent a team of men to hide in the bushes to see what happened after the sun had set. Only the bravest men would agree to go but this handful of worthies did their master's bidding and hid amongst the bushes. Darkness fell and at first all they could hear was the soft whistle of the wind in the trees. But then a song drifted across from the direction of the stones.

> Calally Castle built on a height,
> Up in the day, down in the night,
> Build it down in the Shepherd's Shaw,
> It will stand for ever and never fa'.*

Accounts of what happened next differ. Some say that the song came from the rocks of the walls themselves, which began to shiver and one by one raised themselves from their foundations and toppled on to the ground until not one was left in its place.

Others say that out of the shadows came a wild boar, singing and walking on its hind legs, which grabbed the stones and hurled them across the mound.

Still others say it was a troop of fairies that moved the stones.

Whichever way it was, the men, hiding in the bushes, were sure they were in the presence of the supernatural and fled down the hill, refusing ever to go there again.

Nobody would lay another stone in the building of that castle, and the lord had to admit defeat. The lady had her way and the castle was eventually built down the valley in Shepherd's Shaw, where the remains of it still stand today.

* Taken from Richardson's *A Local Historian's Table Book*.

What was it that refused to allow the building of the castle on the hill? Was it the spirits of old, that did not want their place defiled or was it the wily wife of the lord whose servant dressed in a boar's costume to do her bidding?

THE CHANCER

Staward Peel, near Hexham, is a hidden, dramatic place, standing on a steep wooded promontory in a bend in the Allen River. It has been both fortress and hermitage. You can walk down the Allen to the Tyne valley, where most of the action in this story takes place.

Dickie was a border reiver and charming chancer. He lived at Staward Pele, which had been in turns a Roman temple, a fortress and a retreat for monks, situated on the top of a high gorge above the Allen River. An odd place you might think for a young rogue but a fine one too, for it was hard to approach the place unnoticed and there was always the king's forest in which to hide. Living there also gave Dickie a natural way with animals, which was very handy in his trade as he wasn't interested in blood, just gentle thieving.

One day Dickie set off from Staward Peel towards Newcastle, a good hike by any standards but he was hoping for some rich pickings on the way. Just outside the city at Denton Burn he noticed a couple of fine oxen in a field. They were red and cream coloured with good horns and straight backs. He clocked them and thought how they would fetch a pretty price. Being Dickie, he didn't rush and sauntered on to Newcastle, where he drank with a trusted friend, offering some small recompense for a bit of 'storytelling' he might do the following day. When it was dark, Dickie returned to the field, gently opened the gate and walked up to the oxen, calling them softly. The beasts trusted him immediately and ambled, without fuss, out of the gate and down the road. Dickie pulled the gate shut with a smile on his face and walked westwards, intent on putting as many miles between him and Denton Burn as he could before the sun rose.

The farmer woke to find his field empty and his precious beasts missing. Those oxen were his pride and joy, and the little red-faced man saddled his horse and set out immediately to search for them. He thought west was the most likely direction for a thief and travelled rapidly along the road. He soon met a chap who said he was a pedlar who had just travelled down from the borders. When asked about the red and cream oxen, the pedlar replied, 'If I'm not mistaken, I saw a couple of beasts matching that description heading towards Morpeth not more than a couple of hours ago!' Thanking him kindly, the farmer changed direction and rode off rapidly to the north, whilst the pedlar nodded westwards towards the distant Dickie and felt the warm glow of the coins in his pocket.

Four days later Dickie arrived at Lanercost, a good way towards the market at Carlisle. There he passed a man on a beautiful chestnut mare. The man's eyes fell on the two oxen and he said,

'They're as fine a pair of oxen as I have seen in a long while.'

'Yes,' replied Dickie, 'my pride and joy, but unfortunately I have no longer any space to keep them, so I'm off to sell them in the market in Carlisle.' The farmer, eyeing up a good, quick bargain, invited Dickie over to his house to discuss a deal. Over a glass or two of whiskey, a price was agreed.

Just as Dickie was leaving, he turned to the famer and said, 'A beautiful mare you have there, would you consider selling her? I have need of a horse just now.'

'There's nothing on earth that would make me sell her,' said the farmer, 'as long as I'm alive, she will be with me; better than any wife!'

Dickie nodded. 'Need to be careful with a beauty like that: a lot of thieves about. Do you keep her under lock and key?'

'Oh no, better than that,' said the farmer, 'I keep her in my house; she has a stall in my bedroom. I go to sleep listening to the sweet music of her chomping hay at night.'

'Still, you'd need a good lock,' said Dickie, whose heart was beginning to sink at the magnitude of this challenge.

'Oh, I have that,' said the farmer, who took a large iron object out of his pocket, which he proudly showed to Dickie, explaining in intricate detail exactly how it worked.

'You should be alright then,' said Dickie as he rose to leave with a pocket full of money and a smile on his face.

The next morning, when the farmer awoke, he found his mare gone and its blankets strewn all over the floor to soften the sound of the animal's hooves as she was led away.

Well, Dickie did have a way with animals! But he took no chances and he rode the fine mare towards Staward Peel and the safety of his home. On reaching Haltwhistle, just a few miles from his destination, who did he meet on the road but a very angry looking red-faced farmer.

'Have you seen a couple of red and cream oxen?' The farmer shouted up to the man riding the chestnut mare.

Dickie looked at the farmer, astonished by his own good fortune. 'You look weary,' he said.

'Weary, I'm done in. Someone stole my oxen and I was hoodwinked into riding north to look for them. My nag was lamed on the way and now my shoes are quite worn though with walking!'

'Well, I've seen a couple of oxen bearing that description just an hour's ride from here at a farm near Lanercost.' Dickie gave the farmer a description of the place and how to get there.

'Would you be so good as to sell me your horse? I don't think I can walk another step,' said the red-faced man.

'Reluctant to do that,' said Dickie, 'she's the best of mares and my good companion into the bargain. But I can see your need, so if the price was agreeable and there was the promise of a good home, I might consider it.'

After a little wrangling, a deal was made that was indeed very agreeable to Dickie. He sauntered off down the road with both of his pockets brim full of money.

The red-faced farmer mounted his new mare and rode hurriedly off to Lanercost.

When they met, the two farmers yelled at each other, accusing one another of the theft of their precious and most loved beasts. Then suddenly, at almost the same instant, it dawned on them what had happened. They had both been duped by a most unscrupulous rogue. Despite themselves, they began to laugh at this most audacious of trickery.

They settled themselves down for a good long whiskey together and plotted how they would get their own back on Dickie of Kingswood.

Whether they did or not I don't know, but I do know that Dickie wasn't heard of again for a good long while.

The Pigge's Head

This story happens north of the Tyne between Tynemouth Priory and Seaton Sluice, where the Holywell River enters the sea. Delaval Hall stands proudly above Holywell Dene and is now managed by the National Trust.

There was once a monk who had a habit of taking morning perambulations from the priory in Tynemouth, north to Holywell Dene and back along the shoreline. It was a good walk and, he reflected, beneficial for both his body and spirit. This particular morning he had taken a little diversion through the Delaval estate, when his mind was concentrated by a particular smell. He recognised it instantly as roasting pig. Now the monk was feeling more than a little hungry. Perhaps it was the additional miles he had put in that morning or the thin meals they had been having at the priory recently. But at any rate he found himself walking in the direction of the aroma, towards the kitchens of Delaval Hall. On arrival, he noticed by the absence of horses that the lord was probably out, so he decided to descend the steps to the kitchens to see if he could beg a morsel off the cook. The cooks, however, were all busy chatting in an anteroom, and the monk suddenly found himself standing by the unguarded kitchen table in front of a whole roast pig, the animal's specially prepared head lying to one side. It just so happened that that head was the perfect size to fit in his bag.

At this point, the monk's stomach took over from any sense, and he grabbed the head, put it in his bag and swiftly made his way up the stone flags to the outside world. Now quite obsessed with finding some quiet place where he could tuck into his feast, he walked briskly on. He had only gone a little way when he heard shouts from the kitchen and glimpsed the chief cook's head appear from the cellar entrance. He quickened his step.

It was not long after this that Lord Delaval returned from his ride, to be told that the pig's head had been stolen from the kitchen. Now, this was the lord's favourite food and he had been imagining sinking his teeth into it for much of his ride. He shouted angrily at the poor cook, who said that they had seen nobody save a rather plump monk walking away from the hall, in the direction of the coast. The lord immediately remounted his horse and rode off in a fury. He was just on the boundary between Monkseaton and Tynemouth when he caught up with the monk, the smell and the greasy stains on the monk's bag revealing everything. The young Lord Delaval proceeded to set about the unfortunate with his riding crop, beating him black and blue, and left him lying on the path, half dead.

The monk managed to raise himself after some time and staggered back to the priory. He arrived in a sorry state and was looked after by his brothers. The monk, however, never fully recovered from the encounter, and within one year he was dead.

Whether it was the beating that really killed him or not we shall never know. What we do know is that the abbot of the priory, seeing an opportunity, demanded recompense from Lord Delaval for 'killing a man for a pigges hede'.

It became a matter of honour and Lord Delaval had little choice but to acquiesce. In recompense, he gave the priory a substantial amount of land. In fact, he gave them his estate in Elswick, on the north bank of the Tyne, which became a summer palace for the priors. He was also ordered to do penance by setting up a stone in the place the incident happened which read:

Now at this day, while years roll on,
And the knight doth coldly lie,

The stone doth stand on the silent land,

To tellen the strangers nigh,

That a horrid dede for a pig his hede

Did thence to heavenward cry.*

This stone, or rood, now stands in the grounds of Tynemouth Priory, with all signs of the engraving worn away.

THE LANG PACK

Bellingham is a small town in the borders, not far from Keilder Water. In the centre of the town is St Cuthbert's church, which has a flat tombstone in the graveyard, accompanied by a wooden sign saying, 'The Lang Pack'. This tells a story which goes back to 1723. A certain Colonel Ridley returned from India a wealthy man and bought Lee Hall just south of Bellingham. He spent the summers in the hall and filled it with fine furniture and antique silvers. In the winters he would retire with his family to London, leaving the Northumbrian residence staffed only by a maid called Alice and two men: an older man called Richard and a younger one called Edward. These men threshed the corn and looked after the cattle. The story was originally written down by James Hogg in 1817.

One afternoon Alice, the maid of Lee Hall, was darning a hole in a sock when there was a knock at the door. On answering it, she found a pedlar standing in front of her holding a very large bag. It was not uncommon to have pedlars call by selling their wares but this fellow was unusually young and good-looking and managed to charm his way into the house. He said that he had cloths that he had bought in London and wished to sell in the markets, and he wondered if there might be the possibility of a bed for the night. Alice refused, saying that she had been told not to entertain anyone that she did not know.

* Taken from M.C. Balfour and N.W. Thomas, *Northumberland: County Folklore.*

The pedlar asked if he might at least leave his bag as it was getting late and he did not want to carry such a heavy load whilst he searched for other accommodation. She agreed to this reluctantly and took him to the parlour, where she showed him a place he could leave it. The pedlar laid the bag across two chairs in the corner of the room.

The young man left, and Alice got on with her darning, keeping one eye on the pack, which for some reason made her nervous. One time she glanced up and was sure she saw it move – not much, just a slight twitch.

This really got the wind up the poor maid and she rushed outside to call Richard, the farm hand. Richard came in and she told him all about the visit of the pedlar and showed him the bag lying across the chairs.

'I'm sure the bag is alive,' she said. 'I saw it move.'

Richard smiled, he was a calm, practical man and could not quite believe in a 'living bag' but he was curious and prodded it. 'Feels like bundles of cloth to me,' he said, 'and then again, it is oddly lumpy.'

At this point the younger Edward came in brandishing his adored gun, 'Copenhagen', which he had been using to shoot at birds that were 'stealing' his corn in the threshing barn. He was, however, more enthusiastic than accurate and seldom hit anything.

Edward stood by the bag, staring at it. 'Queer thing,' he said and at that point it moved again. Without another thought, he raised the barrel of Copenhagen and shot right into the fabric. There was a groan, a choking sound and an almighty spasm, which tipped the bag on to the floor. It slumped and the three of them stared at it as a bright red patch appeared in the fabric, which gradually seeped out to form a sticky pool on the clean floor tiles.

Alice let out an almighty scream whilst Richard quickly cut it open and found a man folded up like a baby inside. He had a cutlass in one hand, a horn in the other and four pistols secreted about his body. The man rolled on to the floor quite dead. At which point Edward muttered, 'I've murdered him,' and ran outside shaking wildly.

It didn't take long for Alice and Richard to realise that this was likely to be part of a planned raid and that others would be back later that night. They dragged the dead man outside and propped him up in the coal shed. Then Richard took Edward aside and told him old to stop whimpering and get some help from friends or they were all likely to be dead that night.

By the time darkness fell, they had assembled half a dozen assorted locals who peered through curtain drapes, crouched in closets and secreted themselves behind barn doors. All of them were armed with the dead man's pistols and whatever other weapons they could find.

They waited until after midnight, when Edward, who was beside himself with anxiety and impatient for something to happen, sounded the horn they'd found in the bag. Immediately they saw the silent shapes of men riding through the trees towards the house. Edward let fire with Copenhagen and, to his surprise, a man fell from his horse. This was followed by a rally of shots from other windows and doors which caused three more men to fall to the ground. There was a great commotion outside as the remaining villains shouted one to another, turned their horses and galloped away into the darkness.

The company waited until the sound of hooves had died away and everything was silent. Edward then crept stealthily outside to see what had happened. He found four men sprawled across the ground of the courtyard but decided it was better to wait until morning before moving them. However, as the illumination of daylight came, they found all the bodies gone and only pools of frozen blood left where they had fallen.

The body of the man they had put in the cellar was kept for a couple of weeks but nobody claimed to know who he was and it was eventually buried, together with the long pack, in the graveyard of St Cuthbert's church. It is said that soon after it was dug up and disappeared.

Colonel Ridley was very satisfied with the bravery of his staff and kept Richard on as a retainer to do little else than say prayers with the other servants. Alice left to marry a tobacconist in

Hexham, whilst Edward was made the game keeper and given his own 'gold-mounted' gun. Eventually he started his own farm and gained a reputation as a great teller of tales.

The Thief of Catton

Catton is a village with a single pub, just before Allendale on the road from Hexham.

The people of Catton, near Allendale, were for many years plagued by a notorious but invisible sheep thief. There was not a farmer who was spared this man's activities, losing their precious stock with no idea as to how the deed was carried out. What's more, the perpetrator was clearly a good judge of mutton, as he only took the best animals from the sheep fold.

It got so bad that the farmers set up a watch around their fields night and day but still the thief managed to strike without being caught. What was perhaps even more surprising is that no one had any idea as to the identity of the culprit or where he came from. He became known as the invisible one.

Then one day the 'invisible' became visible. It appears that the rogue would capture his chosen animal by gaining the trust of the beast and carrying it away on his back. To achieve this he would tie fore and hind legs together and then slip his head through the space between. This way the stolen sheep would become his camouflage as well as his quarry, though it might have looked rather strange, an upright sheep walking through the heather!

The thief's greed, however, got the better of him. He took an exceptionally large beast one night; needing a rest, so he propped the sheep up on a tall stone, known as the wedderstone, whilst it was still tied to his back.

The beast clearly became agitated and started to struggle. It then fell backwards off the stone, whilst still bound to the man's neck. The weight of the animal was too much for the man to control and it strangled him.

We know this because the thief was found stone-cold dead beneath the rock the following morning.

> When ye lang for a mutton bone
> Think on the Wedderstone.*

There is no sign of this stone today, though it is assumed that it was an ancient standing stone in origin. Indeed, perhaps this was a contributory factor to the thief's fate.

THE WOLF OF ALLENDALE

The following tale is more reportage than folk tale but has become part of local legend.

In December 1904 it was claimed that a wolf had been seen in the Allendale Woods near Hexham. Flocks of sheep were found slaughtered, some disembowelled, and people blamed it on the wolf. It was causing mayhem and panic. Different people sighted it, saying it was variously black, tan and dun coloured.

Captain Bain of Shotley Bridge said that a young wolf in his possession had escaped but it was agreed that this creature was too young to be a danger to livestock and too small to be the one that had been seen prowling the fells.

The wolf was seen behind Allenheads School, where 150 people tracked it but could not get it to come towards the guns. One group followed it for over four miles but it simply disappeared. Then parties of up to 200 men went out hunting the creature but they were never successful. As a precaution many people hung lanterns by their doorways to keep the wolf from prowling around their houses.

The Wolf Committee was set up to catch the beast, and the renowned Indian game hunter Mr Briddick said that he would certainly be able to find it using scientific methods. But he didn't.

* Taken from Michael Denham, *Denham Tracts*.

Throughout the winter, the hunt for the Allendale wolf continued. Haydon Bridge hounds, which were renowned for their tracking abilities, were put on its trail, but not even Monarch, the prized bloodhound, could not find its quarry.

Charles Fort, who recorded the case in his book *Lo!*, commented: 'The wisedog was put on what was supposed to be the trail of the wolf. But, if there weren't any wolf, who can blame a celebrated bloodhound for not smelling something that wasn't.'

A wolf was reported dead on the train line at Cumwitton in Cumbria but for some reason they decided that this was not the Allendale wolf and it was declared that the beast was still at large. The Hexham Wolf Committee said that there may even be a family of them living in the woods, hence the different recorded colours.

Occasional sightings continued throughout the year: one man said he saw it jumping over a wall, another that he had seen it attacking a ewe. A group of women and children encountered the wolf and were so frightened they screamed and it ran away.

The wolf hunts continued but adopted more of a carnival atmosphere with people adorning themselves in fancy dress, sharing picnics and generally having a laugh and a good sing-song. Slowly the interest in the wolf subsided and disappeared into story. But then something else happened.

Seventy or so years later in 1972, the two sons of a Mr Robson, who had recently moved into a council house in Hexham, dug up a couple of stone heads in the bottom of his garden, a place not far from the Allendale woods. They brought them into the house. After this, strange things started to happen, bottles were flung across the room and the heads moved on their own account from one place to another. Then their neighbours saw a strange creature enter their house that seemed to be half man, half wolf.

The heads, which were no larger than oranges, were thought to be iron-age in origin and were sent to the academic Dr Anne Ross who was an expert in Celtic culture at the University of Southampton. A few nights after taking possession of them, Dr Ross was reported as waking at two in the morning, feeling cold and frightened. Looking up, she saw a strange creature standing in her bedroom doorway:

> It was about six feet high, slightly stooping, and it was black, against the white door, and it was half animal and half man. The upper part, I would have said, was a wolf, and the lower part was human and, I would have again said, that it was covered with a kind of black, very dark fur. It went out and I just saw it clearly, and then it disappeared, and something made me run after it, a thing I wouldn't normally have done, but I felt compelled to run after it. I got out of bed and I ran, and I could hear it going down the stairs, then it disappeared towards the back of the house.

A few days later her daughter Berenice told her that, after returning home from school, she saw a large, dark, werewolf-like figure on the stairs that jumped over the banisters and into a corridor before vanishing.

When Dr Ross removed the stone heads from her house, the strange occurrences stopped. Anne Ross knew nothing about the Allendale wolf of seventy years earlier; however, links were inevitably made between the two occurrences, which remain a mystery to this day.

10

Kings, Christ and Singing Crows

King Edwin flirts with God

In 1949 an archaeologist, Professor St Joseph, was flying over the north of the Cheviots, near the Iron Age fort of Yeavering Bell, when he noticed some marks in a field. They turned out to be the site of Ad Gefrin, a large Anglo-Saxon hall mentioned in the writings of Bede. It was where King Edwin stayed with his retinue on his northerly excursions. It was also where Bishop Paulinus baptised the first Northumbrian Christians in the River Glen.

When Edwin became King of Northumberland in AD 616 he was a pagan. He would spend much of his time riding with his retinue around his vast territory, which stretched from the Humber to the Scottish borders. He would visit the royal villas at York, Carlisle, Goodmanham and Ad Gefrin, extracting tribute, waging wars, consulting his gods and generally letting people know he was in charge.

As part of his consolidation of power, as a Bretwalda, Edwin decided to marry Ethelburhg, the sister of the King of Kent. This, however, brought with it a little problem. She was a Christian and arrived with her spiritual consort Bishop Paulinus. Paulinus lost no time in trying to convert Edwin to the new Christian religion but Edwin was having none of it, being quite content with the divination offered by his chief priest and sorcerer Coifi. Well it had served him pretty well so far!

Then one of those things happened which changed the course of history. Cuichelm of Wessex, one of Edwin's long time rivals, managed to plant an assassin into Edwin's court. The man curried favour so that he gained access to Edwin's inner sanctum. Then one day when Edwin was alone with a single servant, the assassin walked in, drew his poison bladed dagger and thrust it towards Edwin's chest. His servant, however, leapt between his king and the blade. The knife went straight through the servant's chest but the poisoned tip entered Edwin's body just near his heart, causing him to scream in agony.

The pregnant Ethelburhg ran into the room and as she put her arms around her husband, their child was born prematurely, creating much celebration and consternation at the same time. Though Edwin survived, the poison made him ill and his life was in the balance. He called Coifi to his bed. 'Thank our gods for my survival,' he said, 'and make sacrifices that I might walk amongst them once more.'

Paulinus, who was watching, intervened. 'It is not your earth-bound idols that you should be thanking,' he scoffed, 'but the one eternal father up in heaven, he is the only one who can offer you life!'

Edwin looked at him. 'If that is true,' he said, 'then ask your god to restore my health and give me victory over that wretch Cuichelm. If he can do that, I will convert to your Christianity.' A bargain was struck. Belief, after all, could be a very practical affair. Edwin's health returned and he mounted an army to march on Cuichelm. The battle was bloody but Edwin returned victorious.

'Now,' said Paulinus. 'It is time you entered the church.' But Edwin prevaricated, how could he be sure which gods had helped him?

Paulinus sent anxious messages to Rome asking Pope Boniface to intervene. They needed this powerful king on their side. Edwin's wife started receiving gifts: an ivory comb, a silver looking glass and other items of great value and status.

Edwin received a letter from the pope himself, one paragraph of which read:

> We affectionately urge Your Majesties to renounce idol worship, reject the mummery of shrines and the deceitful flattery of omens, and believe in God the Almighty Father and His Son Jesus Christ, and in the Holy Spirit. This Faith will free you from Satan's bondage and through the liberate power of the holy and undivided trinity you will inherit eternal life.

Edwin was uncertain, so in 627 he convened a council representing both sides of the argument. Paulinus spoke with great passion and power about the truth of Christianity, which many applauded. Coifi, his sorcerer, then spoke: 'Oh King, I can no longer see any virtue in worshipping the old gods, for though I have given them more zealous attention than anyone, others have received far more favours from your hand than I. If these gods were good for anything they would have put me forward rather than others. I say therefore that if you find these new doctrines to your liking, you should convert to them without delay!'

This was indeed a dramatic conversion from the priest who went on to say: 'As a priest of the old ways I was not able to bear arms and could ride only a mare. Give me a stallion and a spear and I will rid the shrine of its old idols.'

Coifi's request was granted and he rode to the pagan shrine at Goodmanham where in front of many people he hurled a spear at the sacred objects. 'Now,' he said, 'it is time we all convert to the new religion of Christianity.' So it was that Edwin and his theigns became the first Christian rulers of Northumberland. Bishop Paulinus travelled to the great hall at Ad Gefrin, and beneath the sacred hill of Yeavering Bell conducted a mass baptism of Northumbrians in the River Glen.

The shrine at Goodmanham became a church and slowly the old religion was supplanted, though many of its scared places and practices were incorporated into the new. It took a long, long time before people gave up their old beliefs and some never did.

THE CROW IS SILENCED

This story was recorded by an anonymous monk writing from Whitby between 680 and 714 and happens soon after King Edwin's conversion to Christianity.

One Sunday, King Edwin was striding down the street with Bishop Paulinus, heading for a hurriedly built seventh-century church, when a crow landed on a nearby tree and began to sing. Edwin and all his followers stopped transfixed, they all understood that a crow was a messenger from the other world, and this bird clearly had a message. There was no Coifi (Edwin's previous sorcerer) to interpret the song, and they all stood in terror. Paulinus, seeing that a lot of his good work in pointing people towards Christianity could be undone, quickly ordered an archer to shoot the singing bird. The archer unloosed an arrow and the bird fell to the ground, its message unheard. Paulinus picked it up and strode into the church, where he addressed the congregation.

'This proves by a clear sign that the ancient evil of idolatry is worthless to anybody, since the bird did not know that it sang of its own death and could not prophesy anything for those baptised in the image of God.' Whether the congregation would have been convinced by this we do not know. Would a spirit bird have been particularly concerned about its material death? A little while after this in 632, the 'heathen' chief Penda killed Edwin in battle near his royal palace of Ad Gefrin. Paulinus and Queen Ethelburhg fled to Italy and there was a period of chaos in which Ad Gefrin was burned to the ground. Perhaps the crow did have a message after all!?

THE RAVEN AND OSWALD'S ARM

Oswald became king of Northumberland in 634, a couple of years after Edwin's death. Unlike Edwin, he was a devout Christian from birth, as he had been raised in the priory on Lindisfarne (Holy Island). It was

Oswald who brought the gentle monk Aidan over from Ireland as Abbott of Lindisfarne, and it was Aidan, with his gentle ways, who did more than anyone to win the people over to Christianity.

The story goes that Oswald was such a gracious and generous man that one day he was about to receive his meal when his servants told him that there was a group of hungry people outside begging for food. The servants asked if they should they feed the poor the scraps from the kitchen. Oswald answered, 'No, give them the royal meal and cut up the silver platter into pieces so that they may share that as well.' Oswald himself went outside and shared the food with the poor. Aidan, who was present, was so impressed with Oswald that he seized the king's right hand and said, 'May this hand never perish.'

And perish it did not! When Oswald was eventually killed in battle at the hand of the pagan king Penda of Mercia, his body was chopped into pieces. A raven, spying the right arm, flew from the sky and took it into an ash tree. The tree grew, from that day on, with an 'ageless vigour'. The raven then dropped the arm beneath the tree and in that place a spring appeared where miracles have happened ever since. Such was the magic conferred on the tree that the town was named after it: Oswald's tree, which then became Oswestry.

Oswald's arm was eventually taken to its spiritual home on Lindisfarne but such was its value that one night, under the cover of darkness, a group of monks from Peterborough broke in and stole it. They took it back to their home town, where they made a chapel for its safekeeping. Afraid of thieves taking it, they made the chapel so narrow that a monk could stand but not sit or lie. This ensured that no monk would sleep whilst on guard. The chapel is still there – but the incorruptible arm is gone. Who knows where it is hidden now?

11

CUTHBERT, CHRIST AND CUDDY DUCKS

CUTHBERT SEES THE LIGHT

Cuthbert was born around 634 in Northumbria, at a time when the pagan and Christian Anglo-Saxon kings were battling it out with one another.

The young Cuthbert was a shepherd when his knee became so badly swollen that he could barely walk. Physicians tried all manner of potions and lotions but it only got worse. One day he was resting on the grass of a hill when he saw a strange figure, dressed in white, gallop towards him. Cuthbert was astonished but did not move.

'Who are you that does not rise to greet a stranger!' admonished the rider.

The young Cuthbert was ashamed and uncovered his knee, saying, 'It is because of the terrible pain; I cannot stand, sire.'

The stranger knelt beside him and gently examined the young man's leg. 'It looks bad but it is not incurable. Administer a hot poultice of wheaten flour and milk, and help will come.'

The stranger then mounted his horse and disappeared. Cuthbert shook his head and wondered whether such a simple cure could really relieve his suffering. None the less, he carefully made the poultice and laid it on his knee. It was not even a week later that he was able to walk once more. Cuthbert was overcome with gratitude and realised that he had surely encountered an angel.

A little while later, Cuthbert was again out on the hills with a group of shepherds. It was getting dark and they constructed their makeshift sleeping abodes and turned in for the night. Cuthbert lay for some time listening to the peaceful breathing of his fellows but could not sleep. He found himself drawn to go outside. The night was clear and full of stars and he looked up with wonder into the vast immensity of it all. As he stared, he saw, coming out of the black sky, a shaft of light so bright that he had to shield his eyes. But he continued looking and there within the shaft, he saw a host of angels gently carrying a being of great illumination up into the dark sky. He called out to the other shepherds. 'Come, the Lord is amongst us!' They joined him and watched as a mortal being like themselves was carried towards heaven. They fell on their knees and prayed.

The following day Cuthbert heard that St Aidan, his great teacher, had died that night, and realising what he had witnessed, he decided to give up the material pleasures of the world and become a monk.

CUTHBERT AND THE OTTERS

Cuthbert practiced the Celtic form of Christianity, with its love of nature. It was he who carried on the work of St Aidan in bringing Christianity to the Anglo-Saxon people. He became the most popular of Northern saints with a 'cult following', rich with stories and miracles.

Cuthbert gave himself to God after his epiphany and would go out into the night to pray. One time, he was staying at Coldingham Abbey when one of the brothers noticed that Cuthbert often left the dormitory to go out amongst the stars.

The brother decided to follow him and stealthily traced Cuthbert's footsteps through the sand dunes to the sea. There, he hid behind a dune and watched as Cuthbert walked out into the cold water of the North Sea, until the waves swelled around his waist. The brother saw Cuthbert raise his hands to pray and stand in the water all night, staring out to horizon. Then, in the cold light of dawn he saw Cuthbert leave the sea accompanied by two otters, which first breathed warm air on to his feet and then wrapped their silken, furry bodies around his legs and ankles.

The monk turned and ran back to the monastery astonished by what he had seen but also frightened by his act of deception. He dared not say anything but at the same time could not sit easy with the other fellows. Cuthbert turned to him and asked,. 'What makes you so ill at ease my brother?' The monk lowered his head and stammered, 'Last night I secretly followed you and witnessed a miracle.'

'So it was you that was watching,' said Cuthbert. 'Say nothing of this until after my death and all will be forgiven.'

CUTHBERT AND THE BIRDS

Cuthbert became prior, then bishop of Lindisfarne (684) but he spent much of his life as a hermit on the Farne Islands, where he lived an aesthetic life that was closely in touch with his beloved nature.

As prior of Lindisfarne, Cuthbert heard the calls of birds that inhabited the lakes, the pastures and the wide open mud flats around the priory. In the spring he woke to the song of the lark, the snipe, and the pewit; in the winter he listened to the plaintive call of the wading birds and the honking of the vast flocks of geese. His duties as a prior honoured him but did not call him the way the isolation of the wild places did. In 676 he retired to be a hermit on the Farne Islands.

Here he was drawn to the eider ducks, which conversed with him on his lonely retreat. In the spring he watched the drakes throw back their heads and comically josh with one another, bringing a smile to the hermit's lips. They were his special friends and were eventually named 'cuddy ducks' after him.

But Cuthbert talked to other birds as well.

Not wanting to be dependent on his fellow brothers for his survival on the island, he sent a message asking them to bring him barley grain that he could grow to feed himself. The weather was poor for sailing, so the seeds arrived late. Cuthbert had to plant the crop when spring was already advanced, but despite this and the barren soil, it flourished. By late summer the crop hung golden and ripe. Cuthbert rejoiced, but his celebration was short lived for a flock of birds descended and devoured the plump grains. Cuthbert called to them saying, 'What are you doing, taking food that you have not put in the effort to grow? Take only what God has given for you to have for yourselves.' The birds circled around crying and then understood his words and left his grain alone.

On another occasion a pair of crows was taking the thatch from his house roof to make their nest. Cuthbert asked them to stop but they took no notice and carried on. He then asked again, 'Please leave, in the name of Jesus Christ.'

This time the two birds left. A little while later one of the crows flew back and flattened its wings on the ground before Cuthbert. Soon after, the other appeared and they both bowed their heads to the ground in repentance. One had, in its beak, an offering of a ball of hog's lard. Cuthbert thanked them and used the lard for cleaning his brother's shoes when they came to visit.

Even the eagles listened to him. One day Cuthbert was walking out on to the fells when his companion said, 'Brother, we have brought no provisions with us. What shall we eat?' Cuthbert merely turned around and said 'Have faith in God and he will provide.' At that moment an eagle flew overhead and dived into the river below them.

When they arrived at the water's edge, his companion found a fresh fish lying on the bank. He ran to his master, 'Saying look what the bird has left for us.' He lit a fire and was just about to cook the fish, when Cuthbert told him to cut it into three pieces; one for each of them and one for the bird who had provided it.

CUTHBERT AND THE HOBTHRUSH

This story is recorded as taking place on Inner Farne, but there it may also have happened on a little tidal island just off the main island of Lindisfarne that was once called Hobthrush Island and renamed St Cuthbert's Island.

The great holy man Cuthbert moved out to Inner Farne for the solitude and reflection he craved, to give himself to God. But the Farne Islands are very stormy places, so one of the first things he did was to build a little chapel in which he could pray out of the wind.

It was not long, however, before he found that he was not alone. One day he was kneeling in his sanctuary when he heard shrieks coming from the edge of the sea. He raised himself to see what was happening and looked out upon a hobthrush cavorting up and down the beach on the back of a goat. It was making guttural noises that sometimes sounded like wild laughter and at others like blind fury. The more Cuthbert prayed, the more shrieking he heard. Sometimes there were many of the little beings yelling excitedly at the passing ships. St Bartholemew described them as 'clad in cowls, black in complexion, short in stature and with hideous long heads'. St Cuthbert found it intolerable that a hobthrush should make merry in such a holy spot and asked him to leave, but he merely taunted the venerable saint.

Cuthbert tried to splash the creature with holy water but he forever darted out of the way. One day Cuthbert decided to try trickery. He brought his stew pot down to the beach and lit a fire inside it. He then placed the ingredients for his soup underneath the pot. The hobthrush became curious about this strange behaviour and crept closer and closer. The saint bent down as if to examine something under the pan and the hobthrush came and peered inside. Instantly the saint jumped up and threw holy water over him. The little creature screamed and flew across the sea to the small rocky islands called the wedums, or wide-opens. There, he met up with the rest of his kind.

To ensure his peace, Cuthbert made a fence of straw, facing the wedums, on which he sprinkled holy water in the sign of the cross. It did the trick and those 'hideous little demons with their long jibing faces' never returned.

12

CUTHBERT'S WANDERING CORPSE

THE DEATH OF CUTHBERT

Cuthbert died from illness in his cell on Inner Farne, where he had been living as a hermit for some years. It is worth visiting St Mary's church on Holy Island to see Fenwick Lawson's extraordinary sculpture of a group of monks carrying his coffin.

After Cuthbert died in 687, he was buried at the priory on Lindisfarne, where his grave was visited by kings and bishops wishing to gain favours from his sainthood. Eleven years after his death the monks decided to exhume his body to wash his bones and rewrap them in fine cloth, but when they opened the coffin, they found that neither worm nor grub had touched him. He was as whole in death as he had been in life. They were astonished, and it was not long before the miraculous story spread far and wide.

The monks built a fine new shrine for his body and pilgrims came from all over to receive blessings from the deceased saint. Many were healed of ailments simply by touching the soil in which he lay. The priory became wealthy and this led to some rather unwanted visitors from Denmark, who came not to pray but to plunder. In 793 and 794 bands of Vikings came across the sea in their dragon-headed boats and ransacked the priory, stealing its wealth and murdering those monks that did not manage to flee.

St Cuthbert's tomb was left untouched, and although the Vikings did not return for another eighty years, in 875 the monks, fearing an attack, left with the coffin containing St Cuthbert's body to find a secure resting place.

EILAF AND THE CHEESE

There are numerous churches over the north of England dedicated to St Cuthbert. Many of these may be sites where he either prayed during his life or his body was rested during its long travels after his death.

Fearing another raid by the Norsemen on Lindisfarne, a band of monks carried the coffin of St Cuthbert around the north of England looking for a suitable resting place. They went from Bellingham to Beltingham and as far as the Irish Sea. They nearly crossed over to Eire but were blown back. They travelled to Ripon and back up north. They believed that a sign would be given when it was time to stop. But everywhere they went they heard tales of atrocities and moved on. Some monks died, others had not the strength to continue their journey and their numbers slowly dwindled. It was said that only seven monks were allowed to touch the vessel. It so happened that at one particularly difficult time there were only four of them left. They were hungry and exhausted and each monk knew that to give up now would bring the whole journey to a halt. All they had left, in their basket of provisions, was a salted horse's head and a chunk of cheese, which they had decided to leave for an emergency.

The four monks were desperate to find a friendly household where they might be offered a little something to fill their empty stomachs and a pillow on which to rest their weary heads. The houses, however, were sparse and the people poor, with hardly enough food to feed themselves, so the monks had to keep trudging on. They continued until, completely exhausted, they decided to take advantage of the late afternoon sun to curl up and allow their dreams to take them away.

However, one of the monks, named Eilaf, did not sleep. His stomach was screaming for food and he quietly crept up to the little cart on which they transported the coffin. There, underneath, was the basket in which they kept their provisions. He lifted the lid and immediately smelt the powerful and alluring aroma of the cheese. He intended just to take a morsel to satisfy his craving but he feared being caught so he snatched the whole lot and covered the basket.

He stuffed what he could into his mouth but the group began to stir, so he hastily hid the rest in his bag. The party walked on with Eilaf taking up the rear and frequently disappearing altogether to consume his prize. But darkness was coming and it was clear that it would be long before they were offered any food, so the monks stopped to break into their emergency rations. When they lifted the lid off the basket they found the cheese was gone. Each looked at the other and shook their heads in dismay. They did, however, notice that Eilaf was missing. Turning to the body of the saint in the casket they asked what curse he would put on such a thieving individual. The word that came back was 'fox'. Just at that moment a fox appeared with a chunk of cheese in it jaws.

'Eilaf', they shouted but he was nowhere to be seen. Thinking that this mangy beast must be him, they had pity and removed the curse. Sure enough, not long after that, Eilaf appeared somewhat shame-faced. The three brothers laughed until their sides hurt and that was enough to keep them going to the next town.

From that day on Eilaf was known as Eilaf Dodd, the old English word for a fox. Since that time, Eilaf's descendents were named Dodds, which became the clan name of one of the biggest border families in Northumberland. Don't ask me how that happened – I assume he must have had some other indiscretions apart from the cheese!

ST CUTHBERT AND THE DUN COW

St Cuthbert's tomb has centre stage in Durham Cathedral, and it is said that when Henry VIII's men came to destroy the building they were so awestruck by the saint's uncorrupted body that they left the building alone.

Despite Eilaf's indiscretions, the monks continued to carry St Cuthbert's body. Eventually they headed east once more and stopped in Chester-le-Street, where St Cuthbert's remains were laid for over 100 years, but still the Vikings threatened, so they moved on. Then one afternoon they reached Wrdelau Hill, not far from Chester-le-Street, and the cart carrying the saint's body refused to go any further. No matter how much the monks pulled and shoved it would not budge. Eventually Bishop Aldhun, who was leading the party, said, 'All we can do is stop here, fast and hope that some guidance is given to us.'

Three days later, one monk, Brother Eadmer, had a vision. 'A voice spoke to me saying we should take the body of the saint to Dunholme,' he said. 'Where's Dunholme?' said Aldhun. But the others shook their heads, none of them had heard of such a place.

Just then two milkmaids walked past and one was overheard saying to the other. 'I have lost my dun cow with short horns, she is a good milker, have you seen her?' The other replied, 'Aye, I saw her earlier, she has strayed over to Dunholme.'

'Dunholme!' cried Brother Eadmer. 'It is where we want to go. Can you take us there?' The two women smiled and nodded. 'If you follow us, we will lead you.' When the brothers came to move the cart, there was no resistance and they pulled it easily along a track until they came to a high place full of trees. Here they looked down and saw they were in the loop of a river with crags descending down to the waters below. 'It is like an island,' said one of the brothers. 'It is safe and secure,' said another.

There, grazing on a patch of grass, was the dun cow with short horns and the happy milkmaid tying a rope around its neck. The cow looked up at the saint's coffin and went on its way.

'I think we have found our final resting place,' said Bishop Aldhun. All the brothers ran down to the patch of grass and kneeled. 'Blessed be to God,' they said as one. They placed St Cuthbert's body in a little shrine and set to work building a church out of sticks and whatever materials they could find around them.

Some years later this was knocked down and replaced by a stone church. Sometime after that, this building was replaced by another far grander than anything that had been seen before: the Cathedral of Durham we know today.

And still pilgrims come in their hundreds of thousands, attracted by the story of St Cuthbert, that saint of saints whose feet were warmed by otters as a young man and whose final resting place was found by a dun cow.

13

THREE ORIGINAL TALES

THE POACHER

This story came out of conversations with Coulsen Teasdale from Kellah and other people who had worked farms in Northumberland in the mid twentieth century. Coulsen worked two heavy horses: Tommy and Peggy. The events in the story, however, are purely fictional.

Tommy was tired. His farm was small but it was hard work. He patted the flanks of is two heavy horses and whispered they could rest because it was the Sabbath tomorrow. He went into the house, hung up his cap and his coat, sat by the fire and dozed off. He was woken by a knock at the door and the 'clack' of clogs across the stone floor. In they came, the lads from the farms, the quarries, the mines and even the police station; last of all came Brampton Jonny with his Glengarry cap, who always had a song or a bit of local news to share in return for a drink or a bite to eat.

They settled themselves around the table, got out the cards and began putting in the coins for a game of ha'penny nap.

Tommy's wife, Molly, placed a bottle of burnet wine, a loaf and some cheese on the table with a motley collection of glasses.

'Thanks, Moll,' came the chorus back.

'Hope you lads have got something for the harvest auction at the chapel tomorrow, they're raising funds for the parish poor,' she said.

'Tell you one poor soul who won't be there,' piped up Brampton Jonny. 'Alfie; he was down by the pool last night and gaffed a fine big fish, when that new bailiff Geordie Ridley came and caught him red-handed. You know how Alfie doesn't like to give up what he has got. Well, there was a tussle and that bailiff fell in the burn and when he got out his signet ring was gone. The man was hopping mad and arrested Alfie, accused him of stealing the ring and threw him behind bars. They say it'll take at least ten guineas to get him out.'

'Bloody toffs, think they own the place,' muttered Frankie. 'It'll not stop me taking my share.'

Just then there was a rap on the door. Tommy walked over to answer it. Standing there was a man with a long ragged coat and a tatty bag held in one hand. Tommy recognised him at once as a 'gentleman of the road'. They were regular each autumn, but he hadn't seen this fellow before.

Tommy was eager to get on with the game so he said, 'You can stay in the barn, but hand over your matches and cigarettes first. Don't want my hay going up in flames.' The traveller rummaged in his pockets and handed them over but didn't move.

'Let me offer you a little service for your kindness,' he said. 'Put a coin in here and I'll tell your fortune.' Tommy was getting impatient but he was intrigued. He pulled out a sixpence and put it in the tin cup the traveller was holding. The traveller spun the coin around and watched it as it shivered and settled.

The traveller looked up. 'Silver,' he said. 'Seems like it could be your lucky night: there's silver in your hand.' He gave back the coin. 'Silver in the sky,' he looked up at the moon. 'And silver in the burn,' he smiled and walked off to the barn.

Tommy returned to the table and told the story. Everyone laughed and looked at each other. Molly shouted from across the room. 'Well lads, if there's silver in the burn, you know what to do!'

'You up for it Tommy?' said John Robson. 'I'll come with you.'

The rest of the group scattered into the night, as Tommy and John went into the outhouse to get the gear. They pulled down the gaff from the rafters and the carbide lamp off the old motorcycle.

Harry the policeman always said that the carbide lamp was better for poaching as the light didn't reflect so bad.

Tommy put on his coat with the deep pockets and the gear was stuffed inside. Caps were put on heads and the two men went off along the hedgerow down to the burn. They crouched in the hollow of the rock-face by the pool and waited until their breathing had slowed and they could hear the silence of the night. Tommy pulled out the lamp, turned the valve and shone the bright beam into the dark, night water.

'Looks like your man was right,' whispered John. 'There, what a beauty!' John was good with a gaff; he plunged it in the water, skewered the fish in its belly and hauled the writhing creature on to the bank. Tommy struck it on the head with a large stone and shoved it inside the coat. Then a shout came echoing from the other bank.

'Oy, who's there!' a torch beam scanned across the water. Tommy and John pushed themselves into the hollow of the rocks.

Then, heads down, as silent as foxes, they levered themselves up the bank and were off along the hedgerow. They were almost back at the house before the

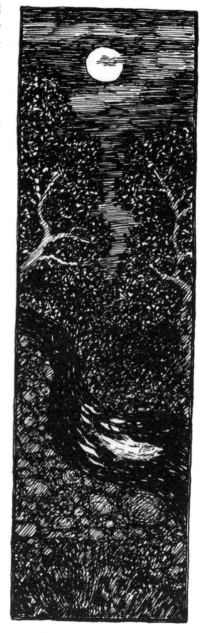

bailiff had time to make another scan with his light. They nodded good night to each other and John left to walk home. Tommy put the large salmon on the kitchen table before he went off to bed.

When Tommy awoke, Molly was already up. He came down to the kitchen and found the fish already cleaned on a large board. Molly smiled. 'Got a big one there, and more than you bargained for.'

'What do you mean?' said Tommy.

'Look inside,' his wife answered.

Tommy peeled back the flaps of the belly and there amongst the pink flesh was a silver ring. 'By God, where did you find this?' he said.

'It was in the fish's stomach; I was cleaning it and about to throw the guts away when I felt something hard. There it was shining at me.'

'That'll be Geordie Ridley, the bailiff's. Blimey, I thought this sort of thing only happened in tales! Wait till the lads hear,' he chuckled. 'Hey, put the kettle on, I'll take that 'gentleman' a cup of tea!'

By the time Tommy returned, there was a twinkle in his eye, he looked across at Molly. 'I just realised what we're offering to the chapel auction.' Molly smiled, 'Don't you be getting me involved with this.'

Tommy took the ring and placed it over the hooked lower jaw of the fish. It fitted perfectly. He wrapped the salmon up in a fresh white kitchen cloth, placed it in a basket and was up at the chapel before anyone else.

There, in the back room, was the minister. They greeted each other and the minister glanced down at Tommy's basket and said, 'Is that what I'm thinking it is, Tommy Graeme?'

'Well,' Tommy replied, 'you know as how this harvest auction is to raise money for the poor of the parish. Well there is one poor blighter, Alfie, behind bars at the moment and I was wondering if whatever we got for this beauty,' Tommy unwrapped the fish from the cloth and continued. 'We could use to ease Alfie out of jail?'

The minister smiled. Tommy and his family had been supporters of the chapel for many years and quite a few generations. He nodded, 'Don't see why there should be a problem with that, you got quite a prize there, shouldn't be surprised if it fetches a pretty price.' The minister winked, 'probably best if we keep it covered, it's an anonymous auction after all!'

The clergyman took the fish and laid it on the offering table in the church hall. It was the first item there.

Not long after that, people started arriving with their goods: knitted jumpers and socks, pies and pasties, chutneys and jams, cakes and biscuits, puzzles and trinkets, pig's trotters and vegetables. The minister set them all out carefully, with the salmon wrapped in its white cloth in one corner.

People arrived and soon the hall was full to capacity. One of the last was Geordie Ridley, the new bailiff, who tucked himself in at the back. The minister welcomed everyone, thanking them for their offerings to this the harvest auction and reminding them that all items were given anonymously and with great generosity of spirit. He was sure that this was the biggest and best assortment of goods he had ever known and would raise a fine sum to help the parish poor.

'Now let's proceed,' he said, placing his gavel and block in front of him. 'What am I bid for this beautifully knitted child's woollen jacket, which I am sure will be most treasured in the winter to come?'

Slowly the things disappeared from the table with six pence for this, half a crown for that and even a pound or two for some of the fine knitted goods. Only one thing remained on the table.

'Now,' he said, 'for our last item.' He raised the salmon on to a little plinth and peeled back the cloth to reveal its hooked jaw with the gleaming ring placed over it.

'Who will bid me a pound for this fine beast?' Geordie Ridley stood to get a better view and suddenly saw that in front of him was not only a salmon, surely poached, but his ring. He raised his hand to protest.

'A pound bid by Geordie Ridley over there,' said the minister. Geordie wanted to shout out that it was his ring, but when he looked around, he was reminded he was in a hall of God and everyone seemed very content with how things were.

'Who'll bid two pounds?' continued the minister.

Tommy's hand went up. Everyone's head looked around surprised.

'And three?' said the minister.

Geordie Ridley put his hand up again.

'Very generous,' said the minister. 'Who will bid me four pounds?'

John Robson's hand was raised. People's heads swivelled in amazement, four pounds for a salmon? And suddenly everyone understood what was happening.

'Five pounds, who'll give me five pounds, remember the money is going to the parish poor.'

In frustration, the bailiff's hand went up again. He, too, was beginning to realise the game was a trap.

Slowly the price mounted until it came to ten pounds, with different members of the 'card' gang raising their hands for impossible amounts of money they could never afford and everyone knew it.

'Who'll give me ten pounds?' the minister said. Tommy's hand went up again. There was a silent gasp in the hall. It could ruin him!

'Am I bid ten guineas?' the minister almost whispered the words. The atmosphere in the hall was so tense.

At the back of the hall Geordie Ridley hesitantly raised his hand for the last time.

'Going, going, gone to Geordie Ridley in the back and blessings to you, sir,' cried the minister.

The hall erupted into a wild applause, which it has to be said, was mostly of relief. Slowly people took their bits and pieces.

The red-faced Geordie Ridley was first to leave, clutching on to his fish and firmly pushing the precious signet ring back on to his finger.

When all were departed, Tommy went quietly to see the minister, who slipped the ten guineas into his hand and said: 'Make sure you tell Alfie that I expect to see him in chapel next Sunday!'

The Gift of the Stone

There were two artefacts which became the main inspirations for the tale: firstly a curious gravestone on the abbey floor which was decorated with a pair of scissors – a women's symbol in a male preserve; secondly a stone, called the Irish Stone, which had been held by a local woman and was now lost, but had known healing properties.

Hannah's mother died in childbirth, which meant that the care of both her and her older brother was in the hands of her father. He was a stonemason and a quarryman as well as keeping a few cattle and sheep on the common land at the foot of the hill. Hannah did much of the work in the house and looked after the beasts when her father was away working with the stones. She had to cook and clean and heat the bathwater for when he returned with dust in his hair and face. There was never an easy relationship between Hannah and her brother. There was an unspoken resentment that she was responsible for their mother's death. They avoided each other as much as they could.

When Hannah was fourteen, her father said, 'It's time for me to give you something, my lass. I know your mother would have wanted you to have it, if she had lived long enough to see your face.' He took her through the trees above the Shildon Burn to where he quarried the sandstone used for the monastery buildings. 'I keep it safe away from prying eyes. Tell nobody what you see today, especially not that brother of yours, this is between thee and me and the spirit of your good mother, bless her soul.'

In the corner of the quarry was a dark entrance, overhung with cut sandstone rock. Hannah's father lit a candle. 'I'm the only one that goes in here.' He led her inside; they both crawled on hands and knees down a narrow passage, the candle flame flickering. After a while the passage opened into a cavern, sparkling with fluorspar crystals. Hannah gasped. She stood still and let her eyes wander round, taking it all in. Then her father pointed to a stone standing on a little ledge. 'Here, take the candle,' he said. She walked over and very carefully picked it up. The stone was about the size of a baby's fist. It was neither shiny nor particularly special to look at, but immediately as she held it she shivered, like there was a current running through her, strangely exciting and calming at the same time.

He smiled, 'you can feel it, eh? Thought you would.' They crawled out of the cavern into the sunlight, eyes blinking. Her father lit his clay pipe, then pulled a soft leather pouch out of his bag.

'Place it in here,' he said.

'It's yours now. Keep it until you know what to do with it and pass it on when the time is right.'

'But what ...?' said Hannah.

'No, don't ask any questions, just let it tell you itself. They call it the Irish Stone; it has some kind of enchantment, but it was your mother used it, not I. There's a note in the pouch.' Hannah unfolded it. 'Hold me but never let me touch the ground,' was all it said. She folded the note and put it back, then held the stone in her hands. Her father watched, 'You'll have to learn its tricks yourself; there's only certain ones can make it work.'

Hannah was seventeen when the reivers came. They were seldom this far south, so people were unprepared. They rode through the mist, spreading out over the valley. People panicked and ran to any stronghold they could find, taking whatever beasts they could round up with them. Hannah was on her own with her father's few cattle when one of the steel bonnets appeared through the mist. He was a young lad, his face soft, woman-like. He raised his lance and started to steer the cattle up the hill and away from her. Hannah stood firm.

'You'll not take her; tha's my father's milk cow.' The young man laughed and carried on chivvying the animal.

'I said you'll not take her, you'll have to take me first!'

He bent down to grab her and she slapped him around the cheek.

'Hey, you're a fiery one,' and he bent down again. This time she bit into the back of his hand, drawing blood. For a moment their eyes caught one another and Hannah felt strangely drawn to him, she hadn't been quite so close to a man like that before.

'I'll leave this one,' he said 'but I'll be back.'

True to his word, he did come back but this time without lance or horse. He came in the darkness of night with only charm and sweet words. Hannah resisted him at first. 'They'll kill us if they find us together,' she said, 'you from over the valley, thieving our cattle.' But he was persistent and gently rebutted her words. The truth was she liked him. He had more fire in him than the lads who lived around her and she didn't want to resist. The two became impossible lovers and for a while she knew the sweetness of it. Then, one evening he told her that one of his people had seen them, suspected what was going on and that he was in danger. He said he would come very soon and they would run away together.

The next evening he didn't turn up. And the next and the next; she knew that she wouldn't see him again. It was not long after that that she discovered that she was carrying his child. Her belly slowly swelled and she kept it a secret until her loose clothes would no longer hide it. Her father and brother quizzed her as to who was the father but she wouldn't tell. Her father nodded his head and let her be. There had been too much strife in his life to make more from this one. Her brother taunted her.

The baby was born, a little girl, and there was tension in the household and gossip in the village. Hannah felt worried for her daughter and some days she put the stone round her neck for protection. Then, late one afternoon in early spring when her daughter was barely a few weeks old, her brother rushed into the kitchen and grabbed it from her arms.

'I know who the father of that child is: it's yon reiver!' he shouted. There was a wild fury in his eyes, an intense hatred that scared her. 'You were seen by the carter over on Ramshaw Fell, I'll not have a child of that family in my house, it were better dead and I'll make sure of that!'

He ran out of the house, baby in his arm and knife in his hand, and jumped on a borrowed horse. Hannah ran after him only to see him disappear over to the woods above the abbey. The brother rode deep into the tangle of oak, elm and bramble, anger seething through his veins. He found himself in a dark place beneath an old spreading oak. This would do; he dismounted, holding his knife to the baby's throat, but whatever anger there was in him was not enough to draw the blade. He dropped the knife and shoved the baby between the roots; the cold night and the beasts would do his job for him.

Hannah searched and searched for her baby but it was the following day before she found the place where she had been left. She knew it by her child's bonnet snagged on the branch of the oak but there was no child. Her brother had either hidden the body or wild animals had taken it; either way it was hopeless. She dragged herself back to her little wooden dwelling, she looked for her brother, she wanted to scream at him to bring her baby back but he was nowhere to be seen. She wept, it seemed, for ever, with the sad, silent face of her father looking on.

The evening that the child was left under the oak was also the evening that a small band of Brothers from the abbey at Blanchland were out with their dogs for a little hunting, to supplement their meagre springtime food supply. It was one of the dogs that noticed it first. Barking and whining at something moving at the base of the old oak. The monks came closer and saw the animal tugging at a piece of fabric and furiously wagging its tail. One of the older Brothers called it off and walked up to the bundle.

'For the Mother of God, it's a child!'

He noticed the horse tracks leading to and from the place, a knife lying on the ground.

'It's been abandoned and if I'm not mistaken, lucky to be alive.'

The child started to whimper and he carefully took it into his arms. The five monks formed a circle around the held child. Their white robes glowing in the evening gloom of the forest, like a gathering of strange spirits. Stubble grew from their heads and chins.

'Best take it back to the settlement,' said one.

'There's something strange about the child,' said the one holding it, 'here, you take it'. He passed it on to the Brother next to him. The monk smiled and felt immediately at ease.

'There's calm in it,' he whispered. 'Here Brother Aidan, you take it'. Brother Aidan put out his thick hands, he could barely see. His eyes had been sore and inflamed for weeks now. He had a sickness they all knew left many people blind. Brother Aidan took the child and a peace swept through his body, like a bright vision.

The soreness lifted from his face. The fourth Brother, standing next to him, looked into Aidan's face.

'Your eyes, the redness in your eyes, it's clearing up.' They all looked at Brother Aidan.

'It's a miracle.'

'Perhaps we should keep it?' said one.

'How can we keep a child?' said another.

'It must be taken to the settlement.'

Then Brother Aidan spoke, 'I'll not part with it. It's a gift from God.'

'An omen,' said another. 'We'll be able to look after him.'

'Him, who said it was a him?' said the fifth Brother, 'if I'm not mistaken, it is a girl.'

The Brothers all looked at each other embarrassed but also complicit. It was too late for them to carry her to the settlement. The child had wooed them into taking it. They agreed that they would let the abbot and the other brothers know that it was a boy and try persuading them that, for the love of God, they needed to look after it. Of course, the fact that it was a girl would be their secret, to have a girl amongst monks would be unthinkable. After all, the abbot would hardly make them abandon it when he knew it had delivered a miracle!

Before they got back to the abbey, they agreed she would be called Brother Quercus after the oak tree, where they found her. The abbot was dubious about taking in the child, but when they placed it in his hands and he felt the same calm and then looked into the healed eyes of Brother Aidan, he was convinced. It was, after all, in possible danger: a truly lost sheep.

It was agreed that it would be best if the baby's presence was not announced to the surrounding community, given the strange circumstances under which it was found. The child would simply be allowed to grow into one of them. The five brothers were charged with looking after little Brother Quercus. In actuality it was Brother Aidan who did most of the work. It was he that showed the others how to feed her with milk-soaked cloths. It was he that watched intently the women in the surrounding community and learned how to wash and change the little Brother. It was he that sewed most of the clothes and it was he that found the stone in the little pouch hidden amongst the folds of clothing around the child's neck. He understood that the stone was important when he read the folded piece of paper in the pouch. A charm, no doubt, he hid it between two loose stones in the child's cell.

As Brother Quercus grew up, Brother Aidan began to hang the stone in the pouch around her neck. He sensed the calm that came with her when it was there. On occasions when the child did cry the Brothers would burst into song to conceal it from passing strangers and then laugh heartily amongst themselves. The child had, in a way, brought them closer as a community, especially the five.

When she started to ask questions, it was Brother Aidan that told her where her name came from and that they found her under the old oak in the forest. She accepted everything he told her. When Brother Quercus reached the age of thirteen the five knew something must be done. They gently let the nature of Brother Quercus be known first to the abbot and then to the other brethren. There were some raised eyebrows but no objections; she was, after all, one of them, and perhaps nobody was terribly surprised. They could not take her to wash down by the river with them in the early morning. So they opened up the passageway that led from the abbey down to the River Derwent. It was a rough-hewn but mysterious place that had once been used to hide from raiders and long ago abandoned.

They would walk down as a group of six and then she would separate off and walk into the entrance of the tunnel on her own. It had a strange familiarity about it and led to a wonderful secluded spot shielded from prying eyes. Brother Quercus understood by then that she was different and accepted her special treatment.

The Brothers had a habit of visiting the community and saying prayers. At times this had gone a little further than was expected and they would end up drinking a little too much and having some difficulty finding their way home. But the abbot had put severe

limitations on what they were allowed to do. So when Brother
Aidan and two of the other brothers took Brother Quercus visiting
for the first time at the age of seventeen, it was for purely spiritual
purposes. One house they visited was that of a woman in her
thirties. Her husband was away and her two children were playing
in the yard. Brother Quercus was introduced by Brother Aidan as a
new recruit. They drank tea and chatted. Brother Quercus noticed
the woman looking intently at her. There was sadness in her eyes
and she felt compassion for her. The Brother held on to the stone
in the pouch around her neck. Then the woman looked up and
said to the other Brothers:

'The children are out the back. Will you play with them? They
do like you coming.'

The two women were alone together, save for an old man with a
kindly face sitting silently in the corner.

'What have you got in that pouch?' the older woman whispered.

'My stone, my special stone,' Brother Quercus was surprised to
find herself saying this.

'And your name, Brother Quercus,' said the woman. 'How did
you get it?'

'From the oak tree, where I was found,' she replied. The older
woman glanced across the room to the man. Brother Quercus
noticed a gesture of complicity pass between them. 'My father,'
said the older woman. Brother Quercus nodded at him and he
smiled back at her warmly. The older woman then flashed her
eyes momentarily outside, to make sure the other monks were
occupied, and turned to Brother Quercus, looking at her intently.
She said, with urgency in her voice, 'I knew your mother. She
loved you very much.'

Brother Quercus nodded. 'Thank you', she said, 'I'm so glad.'

'And the stone, it is very precious, it can heal people. Your
mother used it, but she only just began to understand it, when
things changed for her. Trust yourself with it and you will make
miracles. Are you ready?' Brother Quercus smiled and nodded.

'Remember to never let it touch the ground and to pass it on
when the time is right.'

Brother Quercus nodded again, 'thank you,' she said. 'I'm happy in the abbey; you have no need to worry.' She put out her hand and very briefly touched that of the older woman before they heard the sound of the other monks coming back.

Back in the abbey, Brother Quercus was filled with a charge that she had never before experienced. Something had happened that she could guess at but didn't fully understand. She took the stone out of the pouch and held it. For the first time, she allowed whatever power it had to fully flow through her. She could feel it speak. She suggested to Brother Aidan that he invite in the sick and poorly to visit her. People came and she would look into their eyes and know if she could heal them. Many came from far and wide to visit the strange soft-faced canon in Blanchland Abbey. Brother Aidan always stood by her side to keep things in order. Brother Quercus understood the stone. It cured infections of the eye but also helped people with seeing in other ways. The life suited Brother Quercus; she had a sense of purpose and the abbey became a destination for many. To relax she would walk up into the woods or sew clothes for the other monks. She gained quite a reputation as a seamstress.

One by one the group of five moved on or left this mortal coil, and age too started to catch up with Brother Quercus; her joints began to ache and her soft face wrinkled like the bark of the old oak. One day, she walked up into the woods behind the abbey and hung the pouch from the branch of an old oak tree. A young woman walked by later that day, picking herbs. She saw the pouch and knew it was hers. And so it was passed on.

Brother Quercus died not long after and her true nature was revealed to the community. It wasn't such a great surprise to the other monks, but it had been expedient to pretend. Brother Quercus had, after all, brought considerable prosperity to the abbey. In her funeral oration, the abbot said that 'she truly had been an exceptional brother,' with more than a slight smile on his face. She was honoured with a stone in the abbey grounds. The inscription is worn out now but once bore the symbol of a pair of scissors, a sign of a great seamstress and, in this case, a great healer and woman of some stature.

As for the stone, the last person, I believe, who had it was a woman called Meg Peadon. She is gone now and whom she passed it on to remains a mystery.

THE PLOVER'S EGG

This story is based in Blanchland, Northumberland, in about 1857, when there was much suffering amongst the local population due to the decline of the once very important lead mining industry.

'I've caught him at it. Thieving! A loaf of bread and eggs this time,' shouted the storekeeper. 'If I didn't know you were his dad, I would have him up before the felon's committee and your name would be dragged through the mud, Jack Robson!' The plump red-faced man pushed young William forward. Jack, his father, took a coin out of his pocket, pressed it into the storekeeper's hand and cuffed William across the face.

'Get in there and help your mother.'

There were eight of them in the family and they lived squeezed into one room, together with a lodger. The room was in a house in Shildon, just above the lead mines. They could hear the grinding of the lead crushing machinery all night as they slept, three or more to a bed. Above were the wild Blanchland moors, criss-crossed with drover's routes and tracks where the galloways, teams of horses, took the bars of lead to the outside world.

Jack looked up at those paths leading out of this place and sighed into the depths of his belly. He was trapped. A month before, his youngest daughter, Agnes, had died of scarlet fever at the age of seven and now this: his son stealing. It was all because of the hunger, Jack knew that. He'd been a miner all his life and made enough to get by, but now the price of the precious lead had dropped so heavily that it was hardly worth hauling out of the ground. His old mother earned more than he could in poor relief and that was a shame in itself. A lot of the Cornish miners, who had come up from the tin mines down south, had already moved on and here he was clinging on to the land of his birth by his fingernails.

They'd have to go, move out of their home, or the whole family would be in ruins. There was talk of work in Australia or America, but what on earth were those places like? They were just names to him. People said there were jobs in those far flung lands but how he would get there having pressed his last penny into the palm of that fat bellied storekeeper?

Jack picked up his tools and walked to the entrance to the mine. At least there'd been one bit of luck. His team had struck a good bargain and the seam was better than they thought. It was rich in ore. He'd make what he could this next three months and then perhaps he'd have enough in his pocket to leave: Liverpool and then Australia.

He met with the others, George, Robert and Thomas, and they lowered themselves down to the seam. But no sooner had Jack swung his pick at the rock face, than the coughing began. Heaving and barking again and again, he noticed blood in his spittle. Geordie put down his pick and stared at him 'You've got it bad.'

'Bad? It's worse than that,' said Jack 'As like as not, I'll be taken out of here as cold as those rocks.'

And, as he spoke, Jack knew in his bones he'd be travelling nowhere. He'd left it too late. He'd be lucky if he made a couple more years. But down there in the damp and the darkness he made a promise to himself: if he couldn't take that boat, at least his family would. He'd get the lead out of this seam, if it took the last hacking breath out of his body and make a few shillings to send them on their way. Especially that Mary – she was a good 'un, she deserved the chance of a better life.

The following day was the Sabbath. The family went down the hill from Shildon to the chapel and Jack waved them off.

'Mary,' he said. 'When you get back come and find me, I'll be out the back with the old sow, she needs a bit of company, and she'll not be with us long.' Mary smiled and blew a kiss to her father.

When Mary returned and took off her Sunday clothes, Jack took her up the small path toward Penny Pye. They watched the drovers whistling to their cattle on their long route south.

'So what did the preacher have to say today, Mary?'

'Oh he talked about the evil of drink and damnation to those who touch a bottle.'

'Why don't you come to chapel with us, father?'

'Well child, you see this is my kind of chapel.' Jack waved his hands out across the moor.

It was May; the peewit twisted and dived over the moorland.

'It's not that I don't believe in the preacher but I get peace up here, away from the hullabaloo of the pit and I'm not needing more rant from any man, whether he say fair or foul.'

'Listen, can you hear it?' A bird called a plaintive *poo-eeh* over the fells.

'Yes, what is it, father?'

'That's a golden plover. Some call it the "whistling one"; she's calling to her mate, he'll be over there somewhere sitting on the nest. Hear him? They will be keeping in touch. They can't see each other, so it's a kind of reassurance, I suppose. They are like that, the plovers, always looking out for each other; a bit like you and your friends, when you are playing in the burn.'

'Here, follow me.' Jack held Mary's hand and they walked across the moor, the soft sphagnum sucking at their clogs. 'We'll not find the nest by following her, she is a decoy, we'll go t'other way over there to that little hillock.' They walked, leaving the plover calling frantically.

'Now stop and look down here, what do you see?'

Mary crouched down and saw a cupped nest of grass and feathers with five mottled brown eggs warm inside.

'It's almost invisible, father. How did you know it was here?'

'Been watching them, every Sabbath; they know me.'

He picked up one of the eggs, Held it lightly in his hand.

'She's another nest over yonder; she'll not miss one, and this is more important, beg yer pardon, lass.' He looked up at the bird now calling overhead.

He made a small hole with a reed at either end and blew out the contents, which he gave to Mary, who swallowed it. 'They go far away and they come back every year. Some say they go as far as

Africa, though I'm blowed if I know the truth of it. Recognise each other by their call.'

Jack looked over toward Penny Pye and the drovers cajoling their cattle. 'See, they go and they come, it's what makes the world work, Mary pet and keeps it turning and alive. The plover's young they go too, but they don't always go with their parents. They've got the call to come back to.'

'What do you mean, father?'

'Oh you'll find out soon enough, lass.'

He wrapped the egg in some soft sphagnum and placed it in to bag over his shoulder.

'We'd better be getting back or there'll be no dinner for thee and me and there's precious little of that to be had these days.'

Mary followed her father back down the hill. Heard the rattle in his chest and his heavy breathing as they walked; heard the plover call across the moors.

It was two months later that the Robson family left the single room that they had kept as a home. Their meagre possessions hung in the bags around their shoulders. It was a long walk to Liverpool and the boats to Australia. There was good mining, there they said, and William was still strong, so was Daniel, his son-in-law.

They stopped at the bridge over the Derwent. Jack held Mary's hands and turned around. There was a tear running down his cheek.

'What is the matter, father?'

'Here take this,' he said, and he pulled a little wooden box out of his bag. It was beautifully carved, with an image of a bird flying over the moors.

'Did you do this?'

'I did, lass, and it's for you.' She looked at the box and turned it in her hands.

'Why are you giving it to me now, father?'

'Well child, I'm not coming with you, and this is to remind you of where you come from and to always listen. Put it to your ear and you will hear me calling you, wherever you are, and one day you will come back.'

Mary looked deep into her father's kind eyes and rough, furrowed face. 'But why are you not coming with us? Where will you stay?'

'With my chest the way it is, I'd never make that long walk. I'll stay with your Auntie May; she's in need of company.'

It was now Mary's tears that spilled down her cheek, she pulled her eyes away from her father's face and made to open the box.

'No, not now, when you get there.'

Jack kissed each one of his family, turned and left.

Many times on the journey she looked at the box and was tempted to open it. But she kept her promise to her father. When she reached Australia, she carefully undid the worked metal clasp and opened the lid. There inside was the beautiful plover's egg. She listened to it and she could hear the soft voice of her father and the call of the whispering plover on the moors.

Mary never returned but her grand-daughter did and she had with her that wooden box and inside an egg.

GLOSSARY

Alowe	alight
Bairn	child
Bait	food/packed lunch
Bretwalda	Anglo-Saxon king with authority over many kingdoms of Britain
Burn	stream or river
Childe	the son of a nobleman who had not yet achieved knighthood
Claymore	large two-handed sword
Clew	ball of wool
Drover	a man who made a living moving cattle and other livestock across the country
Galloways	in this context it refers to small horses used for transporting lead
Ha'penny Nap	a card game. 'Nap' refers to Napoleon and is a high bid.
Heugh	rocky outcrop
Hobthrush	a type of fairy
Howdie	midwife
Kirn	churn
Kye	cattle

Laidly	loathsome
Moss-troopers	bandits who operated in the border region during and after the period of the English Commonwealth in the mid-seventeenth century
Motte and Bailey	is a fortification with a wooden or stone keep situated on a raised earthwork called a motte, accompanied by an enclosed courtyard, or bailey, surrounded by a protective ditch and palisade. Built from the tenth century
Reiver	the border reivers were armed family gangs who raided cattle and sheep from other families on either side of the English/Scottish border. This practice occurred between the late thirteenth century and the union of the crowns in the early seventeenth century
Steel-bonnet	another name for a border reiver
Widdershins	old English word meaning anti-clockwise
Will-o'-the-'wyke	a fairy character living over bog lands
Worm	Anglo-Saxon word for dragon

BIBLIOGRAPHY

Balfour M.C. and Thomas, N.W., *Northumberland: County Folklore* (London: Folklore Society, 1904)

Bates, Brian, *The Real Middle Earth* (Sidgwick and Jackson, 2002)

Bede, with Judith McClure and Roger Collins (eds), *The Ecclesiastical History of the English People* (Oxford: Oxford University Press, 1994)

Briggs, Katherine, *A Dictionary of British Folk-Tales,* parts A and B (London: Routledge, 1970)

Child, Francis James, *The English and Scottish Popular Ballads,* ten volumes (Boston and New York: Houghton, Mifflin & Co., 1882–98)

Denham, Michael, with James Hardy (ed.), *Denham Tracts,* 2 vols (London: Folklore Society, 1892–95)

Doel, Fran and Geoff, *Folklore of Northumbria* (Stroud: The History Press, 2009)

Finlay, Winifred, *Folk Tales from the North* (London: Kaye and Ward, 1968)

Frodsham, Paul, *Cuthbert and the Northumbrian Saints* (English Heritage Publishing, 2009)

Grice, F., *Folk Tales of the North Country* (Thomas Nelson and Sons Ltd., 1944)

Henderson, William, *Notes on the Folklore of the Northern Counties and the Borders* (London: Longmans Green, 1866)

Hersom, Kathleen, *Johnny Reed's Cat* (A&C Black, 1987)

Hodgson, John, *A History of Northumberland*, part 2 (Newcastle: T. & J. Pigg, 1832)

Hone, William, *The Year Book of Daily Recreation and Information* (London: Thomas Tegg, 1832)

Jacobs, Joseph, *More English Fairy Tales* (John D. Batten, 1894)

Lewis, M.G., *Romantic Tales* (London: Longman, Hurst, Rees and Orme, 1808)

Matthews, Rupert, *Mysterious Northumberland* (Breedon Books, 2009)

Morgan, Joan, *Tales of Old Northumberland* (Countryside Books, 2006)

Richardson, M., *A Local Historian's Table Book of Remarkable Occurrences*, 2 vols (London: J.R. Smith, 1846)

Scott, Walter, *Minstrelsy of the Scottish Border* (London: Longman and Rees, 1802)

Service, James, *Metrical Legends of Northumberland.* (Forgotten Books, 1834)

Tomlinson, W.W., *Life in Northumberland During the Sixteenth Century* (London: Walter Scott Ltd, 1897)

Westwood and Simpson, *The Lore of the Land* (London: Penguin Books, 2005)

Wilson, John Mackay, *Wilson's Tales of the Border and of Scotland* (Manchester: James Ainsworth, 1869)

WEBSITES

www.faeryfolklorist.blogspot.co.uk

Mysterious Britain & Ireland – The Hexham Heads
www.mysteriousbritain.co.uk

www.themodernantiquarian.com